BY KURT VONNEGUT

A Man Without a Country
Armageddon in Retrospect
Bagombo Snuff Box
Between Time and Timbuktu
Bluebeard
Breakfast of Champions
Canary in a Cat House
Cat's Cradle
Deadeye Dick
Fates Worse Than Death
Galápagos
God Bless You, Dr. Kevorkian
God Bless You, Mr. Rosewater
Happy Birthday, Wanda June
Hocus Pocus
Jailbird
Like Shaking Hands with God (*with* Lee Stringer)
Look at the Birdie: Unpublished Short Fiction
Mother Night
Palm Sunday
Player Piano
The Sirens of Titan
Slapstick
Slaughterhouse-Five
Timequake
Wampeters, Foma & Granfalloons
Welcome to the Monkey House
While Mortals Sleep

2011 Dial Press Trade Paperback Edition

Published in the United States by Dial Press Trade Paperbacks, an imprint of The Random House Publishing Group, a division of Random House, Inc., New York.

DIAL PRESS and DIAL PRESS TRADE PAPERBACKS are registered trademarks of Random House, Inc., and the colophon is a trademark of Random House, Inc.

Originally published in hardcover in the United States by Delacorte Press/Seymour Lawrence, an imprint of The Random House Publishing Group, a division of Random House, Inc., in 1973.

ISBN 978-0-385-33420-4

eBook ISBN 978-0-307-56723-9

Printed in the United States of America
Published simultaneously in Canada

www.dialpress.com

39 38 37 36

Cover illustration by Kurt Vonnegut. Copyright © 2006 Kurt Vonnegut/Origami Express, LLC. www.vonnegut.com

Book design by Nancy Field

BY

KURT VONNEGUT

WITH DRAWINGS BY THE AUTHOR

DIAL PRESS TRADE PAPERBACKS

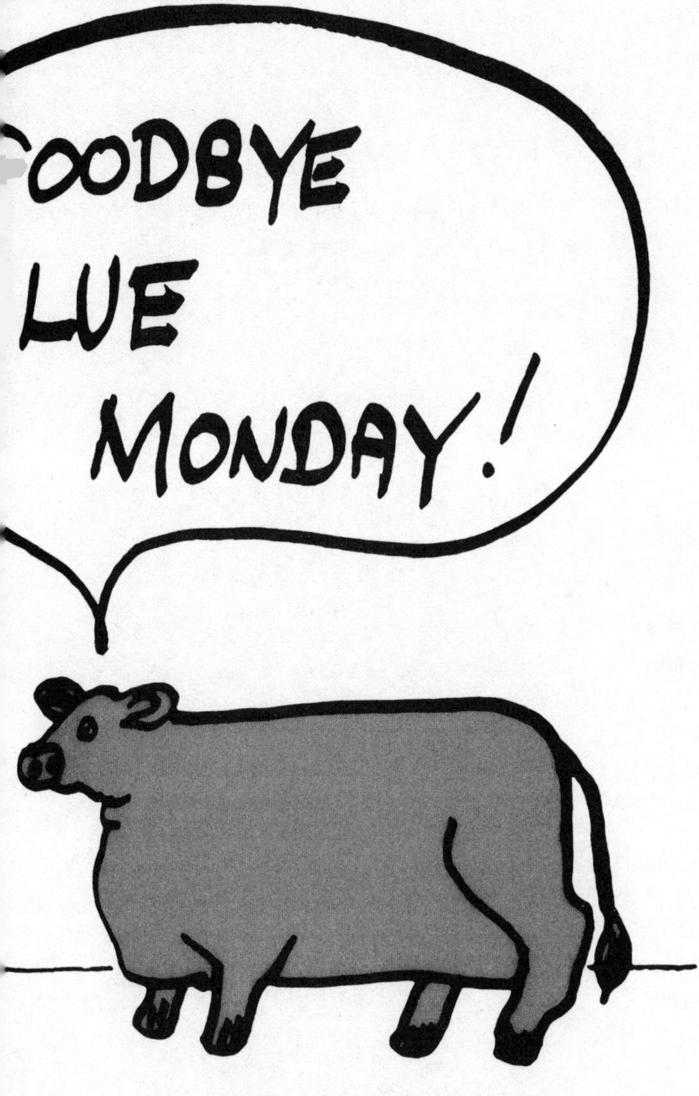
OODBYE
LUE
MONDAY!

In Memory of Phoebe Hurty,
who comforted me in Indianapolis—
during the Great Depression.

When he hath tried me,
I shall come forth as gold.

—JOB

BREAKFAST
OF CHAMPIONS

PREFACE

THE EXPRESSION "Breakfast of Champions" is a registered trademark of General Mills, Inc., for use on a breakfast cereal product. The use of the identical expression as the title for this book is not intended to indicate an association with or sponsorship by General Mills, nor is it intended to disparage their fine products.

. . .

The person to whom this book is dedicated, Phoebe Hurty, is no longer among the living, as they say. She was an Indianapolis widow when I met her late in the Great Depression. I was sixteen or so. She was about forty.

She was rich, but she had gone to work every weekday of her adult life, so she went on doing that. She wrote a sane and funny advice-to-the-lovelorn column for the Indianapolis *Times,* a good paper which is now defunct.

Defunct.

She wrote ads for the William H. Block Company, a

department store which still flourishes in a building my father designed. She wrote this ad for an end-of-the-summer sale on straw hats: "For prices like this, you can run them through your horse and put them on your roses."

· · ·

Phoebe Hurty hired me to write copy for ads about teenage clothes. I had to wear the clothes I praised. That was part of the job. And I became friends with her two sons, who were my age. I was over at their house all the time.

She would talk bawdily to me and her sons, and to our girlfriends when we brought them around. She was funny. She was liberating. She taught us to be impolite in conversation not only about sexual matters, but about American history and famous heroes, about the distribution of wealth, about school, about everything.

I now make my living by being impolite. I am clumsy at it. I keep trying to imitate the impoliteness which was so graceful in Phoebe Hurty. I think now that grace was easier for her than it is for me because of the mood of the Great Depression. She believed what so many Americans believed then: that the nation would be happy and just and rational when prosperity came.

I never hear that word anymore: *Prosperity*. It used to be a synonym for *Paradise*. And Phoebe Hurty was able to believe that the impoliteness she recommended would give shape to an American paradise.

Now her sort of impoliteness is fashionable. But nobody believes anymore in a new American paradise. I sure miss Phoebe Hurty.

· · ·

As for the suspicion I express in this book, that human beings are robots, are machines: It should be noted that people, mostly men, suffering from the last stages of syphilis, from *locomotor ataxia,* were common spectacles in downtown Indianapolis and in circus crowds when I was a boy.

Those people were infested with carnivorous little corkscrews which could be seen only with a microscope. The victims' vertebrae were welded together after the corkscrews got through with the meat between. The syphilitics seemed tremendously dignified—erect, eyes straight ahead.

I saw one stand on a curb at the corner of Meridian and Washington streets one time, underneath an overhanging clock which my father designed. The intersection was known locally as *"The Crossroads of America."*

This syphilitic man was thinking hard there, at the Crossroads of America, about how to get his legs to step off the curb and carry him across Washington Street. He shuddered gently, as though he had a small motor which was idling inside. Here was his problem: his brains, where the instructions to his legs originated, were being eaten alive by corkscrews. The wires which had to carry the instructions weren't insulated anymore, or were eaten clear through. Switches along the way were welded open or shut.

This man looked like an old, old man, although he might have been only thirty years old. He thought and thought. And then he kicked two times like a chorus girl.

He certainly looked like a machine to me when I was a boy.

• • •

I tend to think of human beings as huge, rubbery test tubes, too, with chemical reactions seething inside. When I was a boy, I saw a lot of people with goiters. So did Dwayne Hoover, the Pontiac dealer who is the hero of this book. Those unhappy Earthlings had such swollen thyroid glands that they seemed to have zucchini squash growing from their throats.

All they had to do in order to have ordinary lives, it turned out, was to consume less than one-millionth of an ounce of iodine every day.

My own mother wrecked her brains with chemicals, which were supposed to make her sleep.

When I get depressed, I take a little pill, and I cheer up again.

And so on.

So it is a big temptation to me, when I create a character for a novel, to say that he is what he is because of faulty wiring, or because of microscopic amounts of chemicals which he ate or failed to eat on that particular day.

• • •

What do I myself think of this particular book? I feel lousy about it, but I always feel lousy about my books. My friend Knox Burger said one time that a certain cumbersome novel ". . . read as though it had been written by Philboyd Studge." That's who I think I am when I write what I am seemingly programmed to write.

• • •

This book is my fiftieth-birthday present to myself. I feel as though I am crossing the spine of a roof—having ascended one slope.

I am programmed at fifty to perform childishly—to insult "The Star-Spangled Banner," to scrawl pictures of a Nazi flag and an asshole and a lot of other things with a felt-tipped pen. To give an idea of the maturity of my illustrations for this book, here is my picture of an asshole:

• • •

I think I am trying to clear my head of all the junk in there—the assholes, the flags, the underpants. Yes—there is a picture in this book of underpants. I'm throwing out characters from my other books, too. I'm not going to put on any more puppet shows.

I think I am trying to make my head as empty as it was when I was born onto this damaged planet fifty years ago.

I suspect that this is something most white Americans, and nonwhite Americans who imitate white Americans, should do. The things other people have put into *my* head, at any rate, do not fit together nicely, are often useless and ugly, are out of proportion with one another, are out of proportion with life as it really is outside my head.

I have no culture, no humane harmony in my brains. I can't live without a culture anymore.

• • •

So this book is a sidewalk strewn with junk, trash which I throw over my shoulders as I travel in time back to November eleventh, nineteen hundred and twenty-two.

I will come to a time in my backwards trip when November eleventh, accidentally my birthday, was a sacred day called *Armistice Day*. When I was a boy, and when Dwayne Hoover was a boy, all the people of all the nations which had fought in the First World War were silent during the eleventh minute of the eleventh hour of Armistice Day, which was the eleventh day of the eleventh month.

It was during that minute in nineteen hundred and eighteen, that millions upon millions of human beings stopped butchering one another. I have talked to old men who were on battlefields during that minute. They have told me in one way or another that the sudden silence was the Voice of God. So we still have among us some men who can remember when God spoke clearly to mankind.

• • •

Armistice Day has become Veterans' Day. Armistice Day was sacred. Veterans' Day is not.

So I will throw Veterans' Day over my shoulder. Armistice Day I will keep. I don't want to throw away any sacred things.

What else is sacred? Oh, *Romeo and Juliet*, for instance. And all music is.

—PHILBOYD STUDGE

1

THIS IS A TALE of a meeting of two lonesome, skinny, fairly old white men on a planet which was dying fast.

One of them was a science-fiction writer named Kilgore Trout. He was a nobody at the time, and he supposed his life was over. He was mistaken. As a consequence of the meeting, he became one of the most beloved and respected human beings in history.

The man he met was an automobile dealer, a *Pontiac* dealer named Dwayne Hoover. Dwayne Hoover was on the brink of going insane.

• • •

Listen:

Trout and Hoover were citizens of the United States of America, a country which was called *America* for short. This was their national anthem, which was pure balderdash, like so much they were expected to take seriously:

> *O, say can you see by the dawn's early light*
> *What so proudly we hailed at the twilight's last gleaming,*

*Whose broad stripes and bright stars, thru the perilous
   fight*
*O'er the ramparts we watched were so gallantly
   streaming?*
And the rockets' red glare, the bombs bursting in air,
*Gave proof through the night that our flag was still
   there.*
O, say does that star-spangled banner yet wave
O'er the land of the free and the home of the brave?

There were one quadrillion nations in the Universe, but
the nation Dwayne Hoover and Kilgore Trout belonged to
was the only one with a national anthem which was gibberish
sprinkled with question marks.

Here is what their flag looked like:

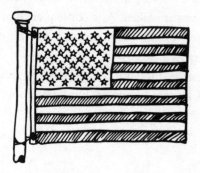

It was the law of their nation, a law no other nation on the
planet had about its flag, which said this: *"The flag shall not be
dipped to any person or thing."*

Flag-dipping was a form of friendly and respectful salute,
which consisted of bringing the flag on a stick closer to the
ground, then raising it up again.

• • •

The motto of Dwayne Hoover's and Kilgore Trout's nation was this, which meant in a language nobody spoke anymore, *Out of Many, One: "E pluribus unum."*

The undippable flag was a beauty, and the anthem and the vacant motto might not have mattered much, if it weren't for this: a lot of citizens were so ignored and cheated and insulted that they thought they might be in the wrong country, or even on the wrong planet, that some terrible mistake had been made. It might have comforted them some if their anthem and their motto had mentioned fairness or brotherhood or hope or happiness, had somehow welcomed them to the society and its real estate.

If they studied their paper money for clues as to what their country was all about, they found, among a lot of other baroque trash, a picture of a truncated pyramid with a radiant eye on top of it, like this:

Not even the President of the United States knew what that was all about. It was as though the country were saying to its citizens, *"In nonsense is strength."*

• • •

A lot of the nonsense was the innocent result of playfulness on the part of the founding fathers of the nation of Dwayne Hoover and Kilgore Trout. The founders were aristocrats, and they wished to show off their useless education, which consisted of the study of hocus-pocus from ancient times. They were bum poets as well.

But some of the nonsense was evil, since it concealed great crimes. For example, teachers of children in the United States of America wrote this date on blackboards again and again, and asked the children to memorize it with pride and joy:

$$1492$$

The teachers told the children that this was when their continent was discovered by human beings. Actually, millions of human beings were already living full and imaginative lives on the continent in 1492. That was simply the year in which sea pirates began to cheat and rob and kill them.

Here was another piece of evil nonsense which children were taught: that the sea pirates eventually created a government which became a beacon of freedom to human beings everywhere else. There were pictures and statues of this supposed imaginary beacon for children to see. It was sort of an ice-cream cone on fire. It looked like this:

Actually, the sea pirates who had the most to do with the creation of the new government owned human slaves. They used human beings for machinery, and, even after slavery was eliminated, because it was so embarrassing, they and their descendants continued to think of ordinary human beings as machines.

• • •

The sea pirates were white. The people who were already on the continent when the pirates arrived were copper-colored. When slavery was introduced onto the continent, the slaves were black.

Color was everything.

• • •

Here is how the pirates were able to take whatever they wanted from anybody else: they had the best boats in the world, and they were meaner than anybody else, and they had gunpowder, which was a mixture of potassium nitrate, charcoal, and sulphur. They touched this seemingly listless powder with fire, and it turned violently into gas. This gas blew projectiles out of metal tubes at terrific velocities. The projectiles cut through meat and bone very easily; so the pirates could wreck the wiring or the bellows or the plumbing of a stubborn human being, even when he was far, far away.

The chief weapon of the sea pirates, however, was their capacity to astonish. Nobody else could believe, until it was much too late, how heartless and greedy they were.

• • •

When Dwayne Hoover and Kilgore Trout met each other, their country was by far the richest and most powerful country on the planet. It had most of the food and minerals and machinery, and it disciplined other countries by threatening to shoot big rockets at them or to drop things on them from airplanes.

Most other countries didn't have doodley-squat. Many of them weren't even inhabitable anymore. They had too many people and not enough space. They had sold everything that was any good, and there wasn't anything to eat anymore, and still the people went on fucking all the time.

Fucking was how babies were made.

• • •

A lot of the people on the wrecked planet were *Communists*. They had a theory that what was left of the planet should be shared more or less equally among all the people, who hadn't asked to come to a wrecked planet in the first place.

Meanwhile, more babies were arriving all the time—kicking and screaming, yelling for milk.

In some places people would actually try to eat mud or such on gravel while babies were being born just a few feet away.

And so on.

• • •

Dwayne Hoover's and Kilgore Trout's country, where there was still plenty of everything, was opposed to Communism. It didn't think that Earthlings who had a lot should share it with others unless they really wanted to, and most of them didn't want to.

So they didn't have to.

• • •

Everybody in America was supposed to grab whatever he could and hold on to it. Some Americans were very good at grabbing and holding, were fabulously well-to-do. Others couldn't get their hands on doodley-squat.

Dwayne Hoover was fabulously well-to-do when he met Kilgore Trout. A man whispered those exact words to a friend one morning as Dwayne walked by: "Fabulously well-to-do."

And here's how much of the planet Kilgore Trout owned in those days: doodley-squat.

And Kilgore Trout and Dwayne Hoover met in Midland City, which was Dwayne's home town, during an Arts Festival there in autumn of 1972.

As has already been said: Dwayne was a Pontiac dealer who was going insane.

Dwayne's incipient insanity was mainly a matter of chemicals, of course. Dwayne Hoover's body was manufacturing certain chemicals which unbalanced his mind. But Dwayne, like all novice lunatics, needed some bad ideas, too, so that his craziness could have shape and direction.

Bad chemicals and bad ideas were the Yin and Yang of madness. Yin and Yang were Chinese symbols of harmony. They looked like this:

The bad ideas were delivered to Dwayne by Kilgore Trout. Trout considered himself not only harmless but invisible. The world had paid so little attention to him that he supposed he was dead.

He *hoped* he was dead.

But he learned from his encounter with Dwayne that he was alive enough to give a fellow human being ideas which would turn him into a monster.

Here was the core of the bad ideas which Trout gave to Dwayne: Everybody on Earth was a robot, with one exception—Dwayne Hoover.

Of all the creatures in the Universe, only Dwayne was thinking and feeling and worrying and planning and so on. Nobody else knew what pain was. Nobody else had any choices to make. Everybody else was a fully automatic machine, whose purpose was to stimulate Dwayne. Dwayne was a new type of creature being tested by the Creator of the Universe.

Only Dwayne Hoover had free will.

• • •

Trout did not expect to be believed. He put the bad ideas into a science-fiction novel, and that was where Dwayne found them. The book wasn't addressed to Dwayne alone. Trout had never heard of Dwayne when he wrote it. It was addressed to anybody who happened to open it up. It said to simply anybody, in effect, "Hey—guess what: You're the only creature with free will. How does that make you feel?" And so on.

It was a *tour de force*. It was a *jeu d'esprit*.

But it was mind poison to Dwayne.

• • •

It shook up Trout to realize that even *he* could bring evil into the world—in the form of bad ideas. And, after Dwayne was carted off to a lunatic asylum in a canvas camisole, Trout became a fanatic on the importance of ideas as causes and cures for diseases.

But nobody would listen to him. He was a dirty old man in the wilderness, crying out among the trees and underbrush, "Ideas or the lack of them can cause disease!"

• • •

Kilgore Trout became a pioneer in the field of mental health. He advanced his theories disguised as science-fiction. He died in 1981, almost twenty years after he made Dwayne Hoover so sick.

He was by then recognized as a great artist and scientist.

The American Academy of Arts and Sciences caused a monument to be erected over his ashes. Carved in its face was a quotation from his last novel, his two-hundred-and-ninth novel, which was unfinished when he died. The monument looked like this:

KILGORE TROUT
1907-1981

"WE ARE HEALTHY ONLY TO THE
EXTENT THAT
OUR IDEAS ARE
HUMANE."

2

DWAYNE WAS a widower. He lived alone at night in a dream house in Fairchild Heights, which was the most desirable residential area in the city. Every house there cost at least one hundred thousand dollars to build. Every house was on at least four acres of land.

Dwayne's only companion at night was a Labrador retriever named *Sparky*. Sparky could not wag his tail—because of an automobile accident many years ago, so he had no way of telling other dogs how friendly he was. He had to fight all the time. His ears were in tatters. He was lumpy with scars.

• • •

Dwayne had a black servant named Lottie Davis. She cleaned his house every day. Then she cooked his supper for him and served it. Then she went home. She was descended from slaves.

Lottie Davis and Dwayne didn't talk much, even though they liked each other a lot. Dwayne reserved most of his conversation for the dog. He would get down on the

17

floor and roll around with Sparky, and he would say things like, "You and me, Spark," and "How's my old buddy?" and so on.

And that routine went on unrevised, even after Dwayne started to go crazy, so Lottie had nothing unusual to notice.

• • •

Kilgore Trout owned a parakeet named *Bill*. Like Dwayne Hoover, Trout was all alone at night, except for his pet. Trout, too, talked to his pet.

But while Dwayne babbled to his Labrador retriever about love, Trout sneered and muttered to his parakeet about the end of the world.

"Any time now," he would say. "And high time, too."

It was Trout's theory that the atmosphere would become unbreathable soon.

Trout supposed that when the atmosphere became poisonous, Bill would keel over a few minutes before Trout did. He would kid Bill about that. "How's the old respiration, Bill?" he'd say, or, "Seems like you've got a touch of the old emphysema, Bill," or, "We never discussed what kind of a funeral you want, Bill. You never even told me what your religion is." And so on.

He told Bill that humanity deserved to die horribly, since it had behaved so cruelly and wastefully on a planet so sweet. "We're all Heliogabalus, Bill," he would say. This was the name of a Roman emperor who had a sculptor make a hollow, life-size iron bull with a door on it. The door could be locked from the outside. The bull's mouth was open. That was the only other opening to the outside.

Heliogabalus would have a human being put into the bull through the door, and the door would be locked. Any sounds the human being made in there would come out of the mouth of the bull. Heliogabalus would have guests in for a nice party, with plenty of food and wine and beautiful women and pretty boys—and Heliogabalus would have a servant light kindling. The kindling was under dry firewood—which was under the bull.

• • •

Trout did another thing which some people might have considered eccentric: he called mirrors *leaks*. It amused him to pretend that mirrors were holes between two universes.

If he saw a child near a mirror, he might wag his finger at a child warningly, and say with great solemnity, "Don't get too near that leak. You wouldn't want to wind up in the other universe, would you?"

Sometimes somebody would say in his presence, "Excuse me, I have to take a leak." This was a way of saying that the speaker intended to drain liquid wastes from his body through a valve in his lower abdomen.

And Trout would reply waggishly, "Where I come from, that means you're about to steal a mirror."

And so on.

By the time of Trout's death, of course, everybody called mirrors *leaks*. That was how respectable even his jokes had become.

• • •

In 1972, Trout lived in a basement apartment in Cohoes, New York. He made his living as an installer of aluminum combination storm windows and screens. He had nothing to do with the sales end of the business—because he had no *charm*. Charm was a scheme for making strangers like and trust a person immediately, no matter what the charmer had in mind.

. . .

Dwayne Hoover had oodles of charm.

. . .

I can have oodles of charm when I want to.

. . .

A lot of people have oodles of charm.

. . .

Trout's employer and co-workers had no idea that he was a writer. No reputable publisher had ever heard of him, for that matter, even though he had written one hundred and seventeen novels and two thousand short stories by the time he met Dwayne.

He made carbon copies of nothing he wrote. He mailed off manuscripts without enclosing stamped, self-addressed envelopes for their safe return. Sometimes he didn't even include a return address. He got names and addresses of publishers from magazines devoted to the writing business, which he read avidly in the periodical rooms of public libraries. He thus got in touch with a firm called World Classics Library, which published hard-core pornography in Los Angeles, California. They used his stories, which usually didn't even have women in them, to give bulk to books and magazines of salacious pictures.

They never told him where or when he might expect to find himself in print. Here is what they paid him: doodley-squat.

• • •

They didn't even send him complimentary copies of the books and magazines in which he appeared, so he had to search them out in pornography stores. And the titles he gave to his stories were often changed. "Pan Galactic Straw-boss," for instance, became "Mouth Crazy."

Most distracting to Trout, however, were the illustrations his publishers selected, which had nothing to do with his tales. He wrote a novel, for instance, about an Earthling named Delmore Skag, a bachelor in a neighborhood where everybody else had enormous families. And Skag was a scientist, and he found a way to reproduce himself in chicken soup. He would shave living cells from the palm of his right hand, mix them with the soup, and expose the soup to cosmic rays. The cells turned into babies which looked exactly like Delmore Skag.

Pretty soon, Delmore was having several babies a day, and inviting his neighbors to share his pride and happiness. He had mass baptisms of as many as a hundred babies at a time. He became famous as a family man.

And so on.

• • •

Skag hoped to force his country into making laws against excessively large families, but the legislatures and the courts declined to meet the problem head-on. They passed stern laws instead against the possession by unmarried persons of chicken soup.

And so on.

The illustrations for this book were murky photographs

of several white women giving blow jobs to the same black man, who, for some reason, wore a Mexican sombrero.

At the time he met Dwayne Hoover, Trout's most widely-distributed book was *Plague on Wheels*. The publisher didn't change the title, but he obliterated most of it and all of Trout's name with a lurid banner which made this promise:

A wide-open beaver was a photograph of a woman not wearing underpants, and with her legs far apart, so that the mouth of her vagina could be seen. The expression was first used by news photographers, who often got to see up women's skirts at accidents and sporting events and from underneath fire escapes and so on. They needed a code word to yell to other newsmen and friendly policemen and firemen and so on, to let them know what could be seen, in case they wanted to see it. The word was this: "Beaver!"

A beaver was actually a large rodent. It loved water, so it built dams. It looked like this:

The sort of beaver which excited news photographers so much looked like this:

This was where babies came from.

. . .

When Dwayne was a boy, when Kilgore Trout was a boy, when I was a boy, and even when we became middle-aged men and older, it was the duty of the police and the courts to keep representations of such ordinary apertures from being examined and discussed by persons not engaged in the practice of medicine. It was somehow decided that wide-open beavers, which were ten thousand times as common as real beavers, should be the most massively defended secret under law.

So there was a madness about wide-open beavers. There was also a madness about a soft, weak metal, an element, which had somehow been declared the most desirable of all elements, which was gold.

. . .

And the madness about wide-open beavers was extended to underpants when Dwayne and Trout and I were boys. Girls concealed their underpants at all costs, and boys tried to see their underpants at all costs.

Female underpants looked like this:

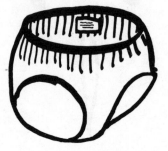

One of the first things Dwayne learned in school as a little boy, in fact, was a poem he was supposed to scream in case he saw a girl's underpants by accident in the playground. Other students taught it to him. This was it:

> *I see England,*
> *I see France;*
> *I see a little girl's*
> *Underpants!*

When Kilgore Trout accepted the Nobel Prize for Medicine in 1979, he declared: "Some people say there is no such thing as progress. The fact that human beings are now the only animals left on Earth, I confess, seems a confusing sort of victory. Those of you familiar with the nature of my earlier published works will understand why I mourned especially when the last beaver died.

"There were two monsters sharing this planet with us when I was a boy, however, and I celebrate their extinction today. They were determined to kill us, or at least to make our lives meaningless. They came close to success. They were cruel adversaries, which my little friends the beavers were not. Lions? No. Tigers? No. Lions and tigers snoozed most of the time. The monsters I will name never snoozed. They inhabited our heads. They were the arbitrary lusts for gold, and, God help us, for a glimpse of a little girl's underpants.

"I thank those lusts for being so ridiculous, for they taught us that it was possible for a human being to believe anything, and to behave passionately in keeping with that belief—*any* belief.

"So now we can build an unselfish society by devoting to unselfishness the frenzy we once devoted to gold and to underpants."

He paused, and then he recited with wry mournfulness the beginning of a poem he had learned to scream in Bermuda, when he was a little boy. The poem was all the more poignant, since it mentioned two nations which no longer existed as such. "I see England," he said, "I see France—"

· · ·

Actually, women's underpants had been drastically devalued by the time of the historic meeting between Dwayne Hoover and Trout. The price of gold was still on the rise.

Photographs of women's underpants weren't worth the paper they were printed on, and even high quality color motion pictures of wide-open beavers were going begging in the marketplace.

There had been a time when a copy of Trout's most popular book to date, *Plague on Wheels,* had brought as much as twelve dollars, because of the illustrations. It was now being offered for a dollar, and people who paid even that much did so not because of the pictures. They paid for the words.

• • •

The words in the book, incidentally, were about life on a dying planet named *Lingo-Three,* whose inhabitants resembled American automobiles. They had wheels. They were powered by internal combustion engines. They ate fossil fuels. They weren't manufactured, though. They reproduced. They laid eggs containing baby automobiles, and the babies matured in pools of oil drained from adult crankcases.

Lingo-Three was visited by space travelers, who learned that the creatures were becoming extinct for this reason: they had destroyed their planet's resources, including its atmosphere.

The space travelers weren't able to offer much in the way of material assistance. The automobile creatures hoped to borrow some oxygen, and to have the visitors carry at least one of their eggs to another planet, where it might hatch, where an automobile civilization could begin again. But the smallest egg they had was a forty-eight pounder, and the space travelers themselves were only an inch high, and their space ship wasn't even as big as an Earthling shoebox. They were from Zeltoldimar.

The spokesman for the Zeltoldimarians was Kago. Kago said that all he could do was to tell others in the Universe about how wonderful the automobile creatures had been. Here is what he said to all those rusting junkers who were out of gas: "You will be gone, but not forgotten."

The illustration for the story at this point showed two Chinese girls, seemingly identical twins, seated on a couch with their legs wide open.

• • •

So Kago and his brave little Zeltoldimarian crew, which was all homosexual, roamed the Universe, keeping the memory of the automobile creatures alive. They came at last to the planet Earth. In all innocence, Kago told the Earthlings about the automobiles. Kago did not know that human beings could be as easily felled by a single idea as by cholera or the bubonic plague. There was no immunity to cuckoo ideas on Earth.

• • •

And here, according to Trout, was the reason human beings could not reject ideas because they were bad: "Ideas on Earth were badges of friendship or enmity. Their content did not matter. Friends agreed with friends, in order to express friendliness. Enemies disagreed with enemies, in order to express enmity.

"The ideas Earthlings held didn't matter for hundreds of thousands of years, since they couldn't do much about them anyway. Ideas might as well be badges as anything.

"They even had a saying about the futility of ideas: 'If wishes were horses, beggars would ride.'

"And then Earthlings discovered tools. Suddenly agreeing with friends could be a form of suicide or worse. But agreements went on, not for the sake of common sense or decency or self-preservation, but for friendliness.

"Earthlings went on being friendly, when they should have been thinking instead. And even when they built computers to do some thinking for them, they designed them not so much for wisdom as for friendliness. So they were doomed. Homicidal beggars could ride."

3

WITHIN A CENTURY of little Kago's arrival on Earth, according to Trout's novel, every form of life on that once peaceful and moist and nourishing blue-green ball was dying or dead. Everywhere were the shells of the great beetles which men had made and worshipped. They were automobiles. They had killed everything.

Little Kago himself died long before the planet did. He was attempting to lecture on the evils of the automobile in a bar in Detroit. But he was so tiny that nobody paid any attention to him. He lay down to rest for a moment, and a drunk automobile worker mistook him for a kitchen match. He killed Kago by trying to strike him repeatedly on the underside of the bar.

• • •

Trout received only one fan letter before 1972. It was from an eccentric millionaire, who hired a private detective agency to discover who and where he was. Trout was so invisible that the search cost eighteen thousand dollars.

The fan letter reached him in his basement in Cohoes. It was hand-written, and Trout concluded that the writer might be fourteen years old or so. The letter said that *Plague on Wheels* was the greatest novel in the English language, and that Trout should be President of the United States.

Trout read the letter out loud to his parakeet. "Things are looking up, Bill," he said. "Always knew they would. Get a load of this." And then he read the letter. There was no indication in the letter that the writer, whose name was Eliot Rosewater, was a grownup, was fabulously well-to-do.

• • •

Kilgore Trout, incidentally, could never be President of the United States without a Constitutional amendment. He hadn't been born inside the country. His birthplace was Bermuda. His father, Leo Trout, while remaining an American citizen, worked there for many years for the Royal Ornithological Society—guarding the only nesting place in the world for Bermuda Erns. These great green sea eagles eventually became extinct, despite anything anyone could do.

• • •

As a child, Trout had seen those Erns die, one by one. His father had assigned him the melancholy task of measuring wingspreads of the corpses. These were the largest creatures ever to fly under their own power on the planet. And the last corpse had the greatest wingspread of all, which was nineteen feet, two and three-quarters inches.

After all the Erns were dead, it was discovered what had killed them. It was a fungus, which attacked their eyes and brains. Men had brought the fungus to their rookery in the innocent form of athlete's foot.

Here is what the flag of Kilgore Trout's native island looked like:

. . .

So Kilgore Trout had a depressing childhood, despite all of the sunshine and fresh air. The pessimism that overwhelmed him in later life, which destroyed his three marriages, which drove his only son, Leo, from home at the age of fourteen, very likely had its roots in the bittersweet mulch of rotting Erns.

. . .

The fan letter came much too late. It wasn't good news. It was perceived as an invasion of privacy by Kilgore Trout. The letter from Rosewater promised that he would make Trout famous. This is what Trout had to say about that, with only his parakeet listening: "Keep the hell out of my body bag."

A body bag was a large plastic envelope for a freshly killed American soldier. It was a new invention.

• • •

I do not know who invented the body bag. I do know who invented Kilgore Trout. I did.

I made him snaggle-toothed. I gave him hair, but I turned it white. I wouldn't let him comb it or go to a barber. I made him grow it long and tangled.

I gave him the same legs the Creator of the Universe gave to my father when my father was a pitiful old man. They were pale white broomsticks. They were hairless. They were embossed fantastically with varicose veins.

And, two months after Trout received his first fan letter, I had him find in his mailbox an invitation to be a speaker at an arts festival in the American Middle West.

• • •

The letter was from the Festival's chairman, Fred T. Barry. He was respectful, almost reverent about Kilgore Trout. He beseeched him to be one of several distinguished out-of-town participants in the Festival, which would last for five days. It would celebrate the opening of the Mildred Barry Memorial Center for the Arts in Midland City.

The letter did not say so, but Mildred Barry was the late mother of the Chairman, the wealthiest man in Midland City. Fred T. Barry had paid for the new Center of the Arts, which was a translucent sphere on stilts. It had no windows. When illuminated inside at night, it resembled a rising harvest moon.

Fred T. Barry, incidentally, was exactly the same age as Trout. They had the same birthday. But they certainly didn't look anything alike. Fred T. Barry didn't even look like a white man anymore, even though he was of pure English stock. As he grew older and older and happier and happier, and all his hair fell out everywhere, he came to look like an ecstatic old Chinaman.

He looked so much like a Chinaman that he had taken to dressing like a Chinaman. Real Chinamen often mistook him for a real Chinaman.

. . .

Fred T. Barry confessed in his letter that he had not read the works of Kilgore Trout, but that he would joyfully do so before the Festival began. "You come highly recommended by Eliot Rosewater," he said, "who assures me that you are perhaps the greatest living American novelist. There can be no higher praise than that."

Clipped to the letter was a check for one thousand dollars. Fred T. Barry explained that this was for travel expenses and an honorarium.

It was a lot of money. Trout was suddenly fabulously well-to-do.

. . .

Here is how Trout happened to be invited: Fred T. Barry wanted to have a fabulously valuable oil painting as a focal point for the Midland City Festival of the Arts. As rich as he was, he couldn't afford to buy one, so he looked for one to borrow.

The first person he went to was Eliot Rosewater, who owned an El Greco worth three million dollars or more. Rosewater said the Festival could have the picture on one condition: that it hire as a speaker the greatest living writer in the English language, who was Kilgore Trout.

Trout laughed at the flattering invitation, but he felt fear after that. Once again, a stranger was tampering with the privacy of his body bag. He put this question to his parakeet haggardly, and he rolled his eyes: "Why all this sudden interest in Kilgore Trout?"

He read the letter again. "They not only want Kilgore Trout," he said, "they want him in a *tuxedo,* Bill. Some mistake has been made."

He shrugged. "Maybe they invited me because they know I have a tuxedo," he said. He really did own a tuxedo. It was in a steamer trunk which he had lugged from place to place for more than forty years. It contained toys from childhood, the bones of a Bermuda Ern, and many other curiosities—including the tuxedo he had worn to a senior dance just prior to his graduation from Thomas Jefferson High School in Dayton, Ohio, in 1924. Trout was born in Bermuda, and attended grammar school there. But then his family moved to Dayton.

His high school was named after a slave owner who was also one of the world's greatest theoreticians on the subject of human liberty.

• • •

Trout got his tuxedo out of the trunk and he put it on. It was a lot like a tuxedo I'd seen my father put on when he was an old, old man. It had a greenish patina of mold. Some of the growths it supported resembled patches of fine rabbit fur. "This will do nicely for the evenings," said Trout. "But tell me, Bill—what does one wear in Midland City in October before the sun goes down?" He hauled up his pants legs so that his grotesquely ornamental shins were exposed. "Bermuda shorts and bobby socks, eh, Bill? After all—I *am* from Bermuda."

He dabbed at his tuxedo with a damp rag, and the fungi came away easily. "Hate to do this, Bill," he said of the fungi he was murdering. "Fungi have as much right to life as I do. They know what they want, Bill. Damned if *I* do anymore."

Then he thought about what Bill himself might want. It was easy to guess. "Bill," he said, "I like you so much, and I am such a big shot in the Universe, that I will make your three biggest wishes come true." He opened the door of the cage, something Bill couldn't have done in a thousand years.

Bill flew over to a windowsill. He put his little shoulder against the glass. There was just one layer of glass between Bill and the great out-of-doors. Although Trout was in the storm window business, he had no storm windows on his own abode.

"Your second wish is about to come true," said Trout, and he again did something which Bill could never have done. He opened the window. But the opening of the window was such an alarming business to the parakeet that he flew back to his cage and hopped inside.

Trout closed the door of the cage and latched it. "That's the most intelligent use of three wishes I ever heard of," he told the bird. "You made sure you'd still have something worth wishing for—to get out of the cage."

• • •

Trout made the connection between his lone fan letter and the invitation, but he couldn't believe that Eliot Rosewater was a grownup. Rosewater's handwriting looked like this:

You ought to be President of the United States!

"Bill," said Trout tentatively, "some teen-ager named Rosewater got me this job. His parents must be friends of the Chairman of the Arts Festival, and they don't know anything about books out that way. So when he said I was good, they believed him."

Trout shook his head. "I'm not going, Bill. I don't want out of my cage. I'm too smart for that. Even if I did want out, though, I wouldn't go to Midland City to make a laughing stock of myself—and my only fan."

• • •

He left it at that. But he reread the invitation from time to time, got to know it by heart. And then one of the subtler messages on the paper got through to him. It was in the letter-head, which displayed two masks intended to represent comedy and tragedy:

One mask looked like this:

The other one looked like this:

"They don't want anything but smilers out there," Trout said to his parakeet. "Unhappy failures need not apply." But his mind wouldn't leave it alone at that. He got an idea which he found very tangy: "But maybe an unhappy failure *is* exactly what they *need* to see."

He became energetic after that. "Bill, Bill—" he said, "listen, I'm leaving the cage, but I'm coming back. I'm going out there to show them what nobody has ever seen at an arts festival before: a representative of all the thousands of artists who devoted their entire lives to a search for truth and beauty—and didn't find doodley-squat!"

· · ·

Trout accepted the invitation after all. Two days before the Festival was to begin, he delivered Bill into the care of his

37

landlady upstairs, and he hitchhiked to New York City—with five hundred dollars pinned to the inside of his underpants. The rest of the money he had put in a bank.

He went to New York first—because he hoped to find some of his books in pornography stores there. He had no copies at home. He despised them, but now he wanted to read out loud from them in Midland City—as a demonstration of a tragedy which was ludicrous as well.

He planned to tell the people out there what he hoped to have in the way of a tombstone.

This was it:

SOMEBODY

[Sometime to Sometime]

He Tried

4

DWAYNE WAS meanwhile getting crazier all the time. He saw eleven moons in the sky over the new Mildred Barry Memorial Center for the Arts one night. The next morning, he saw a huge duck directing traffic at the intersection of Arsenal Avenue and Old County Road. He didn't tell anybody what he saw. He maintained secrecy.

And the bad chemicals in his head were fed up with secrecy. They were no longer content with making him feel and see queer things. They wanted him to *do* queer things, also, and make a lot of noise.

They wanted Dwayne Hoover to be *proud* of his disease.

• • •

People said later that they were furious with themselves for not noticing the danger signals in Dwayne's behavior, for ignoring his obvious cries for help. After Dwayne ran amok, the local paper ran a deeply sympathetic editorial about it, begging people to watch each other for danger signals. Here was its title:

A CRY FOR HELP

But Dwayne wasn't all that weird before he met Kilgore Trout. His behavior in public kept him well within the limits of acceptable acts and beliefs and conversations in Midland City. The person closest to him, Francine Pefko, his white secretary and mistress, said that Dwayne seemed to be getting happier and happier all the time during the month before Dwayne went public as a maniac.

"I kept thinking," she told a newspaper reporter from her hospital bed, " 'He is finally getting over his wife's suicide.' "

• • •

Francine worked at Dwayne's principal place of business, which was *Dwayne Hoover's Exit Eleven Pontiac Village,* just off the Interstate, next door to the new Holiday Inn.

Here is what made Francine think he was becoming happier: Dwayne began to sing songs which had been popular in his youth, such as "The Old Lamp Lighter," and "Tippy-Tippy-Tin," and "Hold Tight," and "Blue Moon," and so on. Dwayne had never sung before. Now he did it loudly as he sat at his desk, when he took a customer for a ride in a demonstrator, when he watched a mechanic service a car. One day he sang loudly as he crossed the lobby of the new Holiday Inn, smiling and gesturing at people as though he had been hired to sing for their pleasure. But nobody thought that was necessarily a hint of derangement, either—especially since Dwayne owned a piece of the Inn.

A black bus boy and a black waiter discussed this singing. "Listen at him sing," said the bus boy.

"If I owned what he owns, I'd sing, too," the waiter replied.

• • •

The only person who said out loud that Dwayne was going crazy was Dwayne's white sales manager at the Pontiac agency, who was Harry LeSabre. A full week before Dwayne went off his rocker, Harry said to Francine Pefko, "Something has come over Dwayne. He used to be so charming. I don't find him so charming anymore."

Harry knew Dwayne better than did any other man. He had been with Dwayne for twenty years. He came to work for him when the agency was right on the edge of the Nigger part of town. A Nigger was a human being who was black.

"I know him the way a combat soldier knows his buddy," said Harry. "We used to put our lives on the line every day, when the agency was down on Jefferson Street. We got held up on the average of fourteen times a year. And I tell you that the Dwayne of today is a Dwayne I never saw before."

• • •

It was true about the holdups. That was how Dwayne bought a Pontiac agency so cheaply. White people were the only people with money enough to buy new automobiles, except for a few black criminals, who always wanted Cadillacs. And white people were scared to go anywhere on Jefferson Street anymore.

• • •

Here is where Dwayne got the money to buy the agency: He borrowed it from the Midland County National

Bank. For collateral, he put up stock he owned in a company which was then called *The Midland City Ordnance Company*. It later became *Barrytron, Limited*. When Dwayne first got the stock, in the depths of the Great Depression, the company was called *The Robo-Magic Corporation of America*.

The name of the company kept changing through the years because the nature of its business changed so much. But its management hung on to the company's original motto— for old time's sake. The motto was this:

GOODBYE, BLUE MONDAY.

• • •

Listen:

Harry LeSabre said to Francine, "When a man has been in combat with another man, he gets so he can sense the slightest change in his buddy's personality, and Dwayne has changed. You ask Vernon Garr."

Vernon Garr was a white mechanic who was the only other employee who had been with Dwayne before Dwayne moved the agency out to the Interstate. As it happened, Vernon was having trouble at home. His wife, Mary, was a schizophrenic, so Vernon hadn't noticed whether Dwayne had changed or not. Vernon's wife believed that Vernon was trying to turn her brains into plutonium.

• • •

Harry LeSabre was entitled to talk about combat. He had been in actual combat in a war. Dwayne hadn't been in combat. He was a civilian employee of the United States Army Air Corps during the Second World War, though. One time he got to paint a message on a five-hundred-pound bomb which was going to be dropped on Hamburg, Germany. This was it:

• • •

"Harry," said Francine, "everybody is entitled to a few bad days. Dwayne has fewer than anybody I know, so when he does have one like today, some people are hurt and surprised. They shouldn't be. He's human like anybody else."

"But why should he single out *me*?" Harry wanted to know. He was right: Dwayne *had* singled him out for astonishing insults and abuse that day. Everybody else still found Dwayne nothing but charming.

Later on, of course, Dwayne would assault all sorts of people, even three strangers from Erie, Pennsylvania, who had never been to Midland City before. But Harry was an isolated victim now.

• • •

"Why *me*?" said Harry. This was a common question in Midland City. People were always asking that as they were loaded into ambulances after accidents of various kinds, or arrested for disorderly conduct, or burglarized, or socked in the nose and so on: "*Why me?*"

"Probably because he felt that you were man enough and friend enough to put up with him on one of his few bad days," said Francine.

"How would you like it if he insulted your clothes?" said Harry. This is what Dwayne had done to him: insulted his clothes.

"I would remember that he was the best employer in town," said Francine. This was true. Dwayne paid high wages. He had profit-sharing and Christmas bonuses at the end of every year. He was the first automobile dealer in his part of the State to offer his employees Blue Cross-Blue Shield, which was health insurance. He had a retirement plan which was superior to every retirement plan in the city with the exception of the one at Barrytron. His office door was always open to any employee who had troubles to discuss, whether they had to do with the automobile business or not.

For instance, on the day he insulted Harry's clothing, he also spent two hours with Vernon Garr, discussing the hallucinations Vernon's wife was having. "She sees things that aren't there," said Vernon.

"She needs rest, Vern," said Dwayne.

"Maybe I'm going crazy, too," said Vernon. "Christ, I go home and I talk for hours to my fucking dog."

"That makes two of us," said Dwayne.

• • •

Here is the scene between Harry and Dwayne which upset Harry so much:

Harry went into Dwayne's office right after Vernon left.

He expected no trouble, because he had never had any serious trouble with Dwayne.

"How's my old combat buddy today?" he said to Dwayne.

"As good as can be expected," said Dwayne. "Anything special bothering you?"

"No," said Harry.

"Vern's wife thinks Vern is trying to turn her brains into plutonium," said Dwayne.

"What's plutonium?" said Harry, and so on. They rambled along, and Harry made up a problem for himself just to keep the conversation lively. He said he was sad sometimes that he had no children. "But I'm glad in a way, too," he went on. "I mean, why should I contribute to overpopulation?"

Dwayne didn't say anything.

"Maybe we should have adopted one," said Harry, "but it's too late now. And the old lady and me—we have a good time just horsing around with ourselves. What do we need a kid for?"

It was after the mention of adoption that Dwayne blew up. He himself had been adopted—by a couple who had moved to Midland City from West Virginia in order to make big money as factory workers in the First World War. Dwayne's real mother was a spinster school teacher who wrote sentimental poetry and claimed to be descended from Richard the Lion-Hearted, who was a king. His real father was an itinerant typesetter, who seduced his mother by setting her poems in type. He didn't sneak them into a newspaper or anything. It was enough for her that they were set in type.

She was a defective child-bearing machine. She destroyed herself automatically while giving birth to Dwayne. The printer disappeared. He was a disappearing machine.

. . .

It may be that the subject of adoption caused an unfortunate chemical reaction in Dwayne's head. At any rate, Dwayne suddenly snarled this at Harry: "Harry, why don't you get a bunch of cotton waste from Vern Garr, soak it in *Blue Sunoco,* and burn up your fucking wardrobe? You make me feel like I'm at *Watson Brothers.*" *Watson Brothers* was the name of the funeral parlor for white people who were at least moderately well-to-do. *Blue Sunoco* was a brand of gasoline.

Harry was startled, and then pain set in. Dwayne had never said anything about his clothes in all the years he'd known him. The clothes were conservative and neat, in Harry's opinion. His shirts were white. His ties were black or navy blue. His suits were gray or dark blue. His shoes and socks were black.

"Listen, Harry," said Dwayne, and his expression was mean, "Hawaiian Week is coming up, and I'm absolutely serious: burn your clothes and get new ones, or apply for work at Watson Brothers. Have yourself embalmed while you're at it."

. . .

Harry couldn't do anything but let his mouth hang open. The Hawaiian Week Dwayne had mentioned was a sales promotion scheme which involved making the agency look as much like the Hawaiian Islands as possible. People who bought new or used cars, or had repairs done in excess of five hundred dollars during the week would be entered automatically in a lottery. Three lucky people would each win a free, all-expenses-paid trip to Las Vegas and San Francisco and then Hawaii for a party of two.

"I don't mind that you have the name of a Buick, Harry, when you're supposed to be selling Pontiacs—" Dwayne went on. He was referring to the fact that the Buick division of General Motors put out a model called the *Le Sabre*. "You can't help that." Dwayne now patted the top of his desk softly. This was somehow more menacing than if he had pounded the desk with his fist. "But there *are* a hell of a lot of things you *can* change, Harry. There's a long weekend coming up. I expect to see some big changes in you when I come to work on Tuesday morning."

The weekend was extra-long because the coming Monday was a national holiday, *Veterans' Day*. It was in honor of people who had served their country in uniform.

• • •

"When we started selling Pontiacs, Harry," said Dwayne, "the car was sensible transportation for school teachers and grandmothers and maiden aunts." This was true. "Perhaps you haven't noticed, Harry, but the Pontiac has now become a glamorous, youthful adventure for people who want a *kick* out of life! And you dress and act like this was a mortuary! Look at yourself in a mirror, Harry, and ask yourself, 'Who could ever associate a man like this with a Pontiac?' "

Harry LeSabre was too choked up to point out to Dwayne that, no matter what he looked like, he was generally acknowledged to be one of the most effective sales managers for Pontiac not only in the State, but in the entire Middle West. Pontiac was the best-selling automobile in the Midland City area, despite the fact that it was not a low-price car. It was a medium-price car.

• • •

Dwayne Hoover told poor Harry LeSabre that the Hawaiian Festival, only a long weekend away, was Harry's golden opportunity to loosen up, to have some fun, to encourage other people to have some fun, too.

"Harry," said Dwayne. "I have some news for you: modern science has given us a whole lot of wonderful new colors, with strange, exciting names like *red!*, *orange!*, *green!*, and *pink!*, Harry. We're not stuck any more with just black, gray and white! Isn't that good news, Harry? And the State Legislature has just announced that it is no longer a crime to smile during working hours, Harry, and I have the personal promise of the Governor that never again will anybody be sent to the Sexual Offenders' Wing of the Adult Correctional Institution for telling a joke!"

• • •

Harry LeSabre might have weathered all this with only minor damage, if only Harry hadn't been a secret transvestite. On weekends he liked to dress up in women's clothing, and not drab clothing, either. Harry and his wife would pull down the window blinds, and Harry would turn into a bird of paradise.

Nobody but Harry's wife knew his secret.

When Dwayne razzed him about the clothes he wore to work, and then mentioned the Sexual Offenders' Wing of the Adult Correctional Institution at Shepherdstown, Harry had to suspect that his secret was out. And it wasn't merely a comical secret, either. Harry could be arrested for what he did on weekends. He could be fined up to three thousand dollars and sentenced to as much as five years at hard labor in the

Sexual Offenders' Wing of the Adult Correctional Institution at Shepherdstown.

. . .

So poor Harry spent a wretched Veterans' Day weekend after that. But Dwayne spent a worse one.

Here is what the last night of that weekend was like for Dwayne: his bad chemicals rolled him out of bed. They made him dress as though there were some sort of emergency with which he had to deal. This was in the wee hours. Veterans' Day had ended at the stroke of twelve.

Dwayne's bad chemicals made him take a loaded thirty-eight caliber revolver from under his pillow and stick it in his mouth. This was a tool whose only purpose was to make holes in human beings. It looked like this:

In Dwayne's part of the planet, anybody who wanted one could get one down at his local hardware store. Policemen all had them. So did the criminals. So did the people caught in between.

Criminals would point guns at people and say, "Give me all your money," and the people usually would. And policemen would point their guns at criminals and say, "Stop" or whatever the situation called for, and the criminals usually would. Sometimes they wouldn't. Sometimes a wife would get so mad at her husband that she would put a hole in him with a gun. Sometimes a husband would get so mad at his wife that he would put a hole in her. And so on.

In the same week Dwayne Hoover ran amok, a four-teen-year-old Midland City boy put holes in his mother and father because he didn't want to show them the bad report card he had brought home. His lawyer planned to enter a plea of temporary insanity, which meant that at the time of the shooting the boy was unable to distinguish the difference be-tween right and wrong.

· · ·

Sometimes people would put holes in famous people so they could be at least fairly famous, too. Sometimes people would get on airplanes which were supposed to fly to some-place, and they would offer to put holes in the pilot and co-pilot unless they flew the airplane to someplace else.

· · ·

Dwayne held the muzzle of his gun in his mouth for a while. He tasted oil. The gun was loaded and cocked. There were neat little metal packages containing charcoal, potassium nitrate and sulphur only inches from his brains. He had only to trip a lever, and the powder would turn to gas. The gas would blow a chunk of lead down a tube and through Dwayne's brains.

But Dwayne elected to shoot up one of his tiled bath-rooms instead. He put chunks of lead through his toilet and a washbasin and a bathtub enclosure. There was a picture of a flamingo sandblasted on the glass of the bathtub enclosure. It looked like this:

Dwayne shot the flamingo.

He snarled at his recollection of it afterwards. Here is what he snarled: "Dumb fucking bird."

• • •

Nobody heard the shots. All the houses in the neighborhood were too well insulated for sound ever to get in or out. A sound wanting in or out of Dwayne's dreamhouse, for instance, had to go through an inch and a half of plasterboard, a polystyrene vapor barrier, a sheet of aluminum foil, a three-inch airspace, another sheet of aluminum foil, a three-inch blanket of glass wool, another sheet of aluminum foil, one inch of insulating board made of pressed sawdust, tarpaper, one inch of wood sheathing, more tarpaper, and then aluminum siding which was hollow. The space in the siding was filled with a miracle insulating material developed for use on rockets to the Moon.

• • •

Dwayne turned on the floodlights around his house, and he played basketball on the blacktop apron outside his five-car garage.

Dwayne's dog Sparky hid in the basement when Dwayne shot up the bathroom. But he came out now. Sparky watched Dwayne play basketball.

"You and me, Sparky," said Dwayne. And so on. He sure loved that dog.

Nobody saw him playing basketball. He was screened from his neighbors by trees and shrubs and a high cedar fence.

• • •

He put the basketball away, and he climbed into a black Plymouth *Fury* he had taken in trade the day before. The Plymouth was a Chrysler product, and Dwayne himself sold General Motors products. He had decided to drive the Plymouth for a day or two in order to keep abreast of the competition.

As he backed out of his driveway, he thought it important to explain to his neighbors why he was in a Plymouth *Fury,* so he yelled out the window: "Keeping abreast of the competition!" He blew his horn.

• • •

Dwayne zoomed down Old County Road and onto the Interstate, which he had all to himself. He swerved into Exit Ten at a high rate of speed, slammed into a guardrail, spun around and around. He came out onto Union Avenue going backwards, jumped a curb, and came to a stop in a vacant lot. Dwayne owned the lot.

Nobody saw or heard anything. Nobody lived in the area. A policeman was supposed to cruise by about once every hour or so, but he was cooping in an alley behind a Western Electric warehouse about two miles away. *Cooping* was police slang for sleeping on the job.

• • •

Dwayne stayed in his vacant lot for a while. He played the radio. All the Midland City stations were asleep for the night, but Dwayne picked up a country music station in West Virginia, which offered him ten different kinds of flowering shrubs and five fruit trees for six dollars, C.O.D.

"Sounds good to me," said Dwayne. He meant it. Almost all the messages which were sent and received in his country, even the telepathic ones, had to do with buying or selling some damn thing. They were like lullabies to Dwayne.

5

WHILE DWAYNE HOOVER listened to West Virginia, Kilgore Trout tried to fall asleep in a movie theater in New York City. It was much cheaper than a night in a hotel. Trout had never done it before, but he knew sleeping in movie houses was the sort of thing really dirty old men did. He wished to arrive in Midland City as the dirtiest of all old men. He was supposed to take part in a symposium out there entitled "The Future of the American Novel in the Age of McLuhan." He wished to say at that symposium, "I don't know who McLuhan is, but I know what it's like to spend the night with a lot of other dirty old men in a movie theater in New York City. Could we talk about that?"

He wished to say, too, "Does this McLuhan, whoever he is, have anything to say about the relationship between wide-open beavers and the sales of books?"

• • •

Trout had come down from Cohoes late that afternoon. He had since visited many pornography shops and a shirt store. He had bought two of his own books, *Plague on Wheels* and *Now It Can Be Told,* a magazine containing a short story of his, and a tuxedo shirt. The name of the magazine was *Black*

Garterbelt. The tuxedo shirt had a cascade of ruffles down its bosom. On the shirt salesman's advice, Trout had also bought a packaged ensemble consisting of a cumberbund, a boutonnière, and a bow tie. They were all the color of tangerines.

These goodies were all in his lap, along with a crackling brown paper parcel containing his tuxedo, six new pairs of jockey shorts, six new pairs of socks, his razor and a new toothbrush. Trout hadn't owned a toothbrush for years.

· · ·

The jackets of *Plague on Wheels* and *Now It Can Be Told* both promised plenty of wide-open beavers inside. The picture on the cover of *Now It Can Be Told,* which was the book which would turn Dwayne Hoover into a homicidal maniac, showed a college professor being undressed by a group of naked sorority girls. A library tower could be seen through a window in the sorority house. It was daytime outside, and there was a clock in the tower. The clock looked like this:

The professor was stripped down to his candy-striped underwear shorts and his socks and garters and his mortarboard, which was a hat which looked like this:

There was absolutely nothing about a professor or a sorority or a university anywhere in the body of the book. The book was in the form of a long letter from the Creator of the Universe to the only creature in the Universe who had free will.

• • •

As for the story in *Black Garterbelt* magazine: Trout had no idea that it had been accepted for publication. It had been accepted years ago, apparently, for the date on the magazine was April, 1962. Trout found it by chance in a bin of tame old magazines near the front of the store. They were underpants magazines.

When he bought the magazine, the cashier supposed Trout was drunk or feeble-minded. All he was getting, the cashier thought, was pictures of women in their underpants. Their legs were apart, all right, but they had on underpants, so they were certainly no competition for the wide-open beavers on sale in the back of the store.

"I hope you enjoy it," said the cashier to Trout. He meant that he hoped Trout would find some pictures he could masturbate to, since that was the only point of all the books and magazines.

"It's for an arts festival," said Trout.

• • •

As for the story itself, it was entitled "The Dancing Fool." Like so many Trout stories, it was about a tragic failure to communicate.

Here was the plot: A flying saucer creature named Zog arrived on Earth to explain how wars could be prevented and how cancer could be cured. He brought the information from Margo, a planet where the natives conversed by means of farts and tap dancing.

Zog landed at night in Connecticut. He had no sooner touched down than he saw a house on fire. He rushed into the house, farting and tap dancing, warning the people about the terrible danger they were in. The head of the house brained Zog with a golfclub.

• • •

The movie theater where Trout sat with all his parcels in his lap showed nothing but dirty movies. The music was soothing. Phantasms of a young man and a young woman sucked harmlessly on one another's soft apertures on the silver screen.

And Trout made up a new novel while he sat there. It was about an Earthling astronaut who arrived on a planet where all the animal and plant life had been killed by pollution, except for humanoids. The humanoids ate food made from petroleum and coal.

They gave a feast for the astronaut, whose name was Don. The food was terrible. The big topic of conversation was censorship. The cities were blighted with motion picture theaters which showed nothing but dirty movies. The humanoids wished they could put them out of business somehow, but without interfering with free speech.

They asked Don if dirty movies were a problem on Earth, too, and Don said, "Yes." They asked him if the movies were *really* dirty, and Don replied, "As dirty as movies could get."

This was a challenge to the humanoids, who were sure their dirty movies could beat anything on Earth. So everybody piled into air-cushion vehicles, and they floated to a dirty movie house downtown.

It was intermission time when they got there, so Don had some time to think about what could possibly be dirtier than what he had already seen on Earth. He became sexually excited even before the house lights went down. The women in his party were all twittery and squirmy.

So the theater went dark and the curtains opened. At first there wasn't any picture. There were slurps and moans from loudspeakers. Then the picture itself appeared. It was a high quality film of a male humanoid eating what looked like a pear. The camera zoomed in on his lips and tongue and teeth, which glistened with saliva. He took his time about eating the pear. When the last of it had disappeared into his slurpy mouth, the camera focussed on his Adam's apple. His Adam's apple bobbed obscenely. He belched contentedly, and then these words appeared on the screen, but in the language of the planet:

THE END

• • •

It was all faked, of course. There weren't any pears anymore. And the eating of a pear wasn't the main event of the evening anyway. It was a short subject, which gave the members of the audience time to settle down.

Then the main feature began. It was about a male and a female and their two children, and their dog and their cat. They ate steadily for an hour and a half—soup, meat, biscuits, butter, vegetables, mashed potatoes and gravy, fruit, candy, cake, pie. The camera rarely strayed more than a foot from their glistening lips and their bobbing Adam's apples. And then the father put the cat and dog on the table, so they could take part in the orgy, too.

After a while, the actors couldn't eat any more. They were so stuffed that they were goggle-eyed. They could hardly move. They said they didn't think they could eat again for a week, and so on. They cleared the table slowly. They went waddling out into the kitchen, and they dumped about thirty pounds of leftovers into a garbage can.

The audience went wild.

• • •

When Don and his friends left the theater, they were accosted by humanoid whores, who offered them eggs and oranges and milk and butter and peanuts and so on. The whores couldn't actually deliver these goodies, of course.

The humanoids told Don that if he went home with a

whore, she would cook him a meal of petroleum and coal products at fancy prices.

And then, while he ate them, she would talk dirty about how fresh and full of natural juices the food was, even though the food was fake.

6

DWAYNE HOOVER sat in the used Plymouth *Fury* in his own vacant lot for an hour, listening to West Virginia. He was told about health insurance for pennies a day, about how to get better performance from his car. He was told what to do about constipation. He was offered a Bible which had everything that God or Jesus had actually said out loud printed in red capital letters. He was offered a plant which would attract and eat disease-carrying insects in his home.

All this was stored away in Dwayne's memory, in case he should need it later on. He had all kinds of stuff in there.

· · ·

While Dwayne sat there so alone, the oldest inhabitant of Midland City was dying in the County Hospital, at the foot of Fairchild Boulevard, which was nine miles away. She was Mary Young. She was one hundred and eight years old. She was black. Mary Young's parents had been human slaves in Kentucky.

There was a tiny connection between Mary Young and Dwayne Hoover. She did the laundry for Dwayne's family for a few months, back when Dwayne was a little boy. She told Bible stories and stories about slavery to little Dwayne. She told him about a public hanging of a white man she had seen in Cincinnati, when she was a little girl.

• • •

A black intern at the County Hospital now watched Mary Young die of pneumonia.

The intern did not know her. He had been in Midland City for only a week. He wasn't even a fellow-American, although he had taken his medical degree at Harvard. He was an Indaro. He was a Nigerian. His name was Cyprian Ukwende. He felt no kinship with Mary or with any American blacks. He felt kinship only with Indaros.

As she died, Mary was as alone on the planet as were Dwayne Hoover or Kilgore Trout. She had never reproduced. There were no friends or relatives to watch her die. So she spoke her very last words on the planet to Cyprian Ukwende. She did not have enough breath left to make her vocal cords buzz. She could only move her lips noiselessly.

Here is all she had to say about death: "Oh my, oh my."

• • •

Like all Earthlings at the point of death, Mary Young sent faint reminders of herself to those who had known her. She released a small cloud of telepathic butterflies, and one of these brushed the cheek of Dwayne Hoover, nine miles away.

Dwayne heard a tired voice from somewhere behind his head, even though no one was back there. It said this to Dwayne: "Oh my, oh my."

• • •

Dwayne's bad chemicals now made him put his car in gear. He drove out of the vacant lot, proceeded sedately down Union Avenue, which paralleled the Interstate.

He went past his principal place of business, which was *Dwayne Hoover's Exit Eleven Pontiac Village,* and he turned into the parking lot of the new Holiday Inn next door. Dwayne owned a third of the Inn—in partnership with Midland City's leading orthodontist, Dr. Alfred Maritimo, and Bill Miller, who was Chairman of the Parole Board at the Adult Correctional Institution at Shepherdstown, among other things.

Dwayne went up the Inn's back steps to the roof without meeting anybody. There was a full moon. There were *two* full moons. The new Mildred Barry Memorial Center for the Arts was a translucent sphere on stilts, and it was illuminated from the inside now—and it looked like a moon.

• • •

Dwayne gazed over the sleeping city. He had been born there. He had spent the first three years of his life in an orphanage only two miles from where he stood. He had been adopted and educated there.

He owned not only the Pontiac agency and a piece of the new Holiday Inn. He owned three Burger Chefs, too, and five coin-operated car washes, and pieces of the Sugar Creek Drive-In Theatre, Radio Station WMCY, the Three Maples Par-Three Golf Course, and seventeen hundred shares of common stock in Barrytron, Limited, a local electronics firm. He owned dozens of vacant lots. He was on the Board of Directors of the Midland County National Bank.

But now Midland City looked unfamiliar and frightening to Dwayne. "Where am I?" he said.

He even forgot that his wife Celia had committed suicide, for instance, by eating Drāno—a mixture of sodium hydroxide and aluminum flakes, which was meant to clear drains. Celia became a small volcano, since she was composed of the same sorts of substances which commonly clogged drains.

Dwayne even forgot that his only child, a son, had grown up to be a notorious homosexual. His name was George, but everybody called him "Bunny." He played piano in the cocktail lounge of the new Holiday Inn.

"Where am I?" said Dwayne.

7

KILGORE TROUT took a leak in the men's room of the New York City movie house. There was a sign on the wall next to the roller towel. It advertised a massage parlor called *The Sultan's Harem*. Massage parlors were something new and exciting in New York. Men could go in there and photograph naked women, or they could paint the women's naked bodies with water-soluble paints. Men could be rubbed all over by a woman until their penises squirted jism into Turkish towels.

"It's a full life and a merry one," said Kilgore Trout.

There was a message written in pencil on the tiles by the roller towel. This was it:

What is the purpose of life?

Trout plundered his pockets for a pen or pencil. He had an answer to the question. But he had nothing to write with, not even a burnt match. So he left the question unanswered, but here is what he would have written, if he had found anything to write with:

> *To be*
> *the eyes*
> *and ears*
> *and conscience*
> *of the Creator of the Universe,*
> *you fool.*

When Trout headed back for his seat in the theater, he played at being the eyes and ears and conscience of the Creator of the Universe. He sent messages by telepathy to the Creator, wherever He was. He reported that the men's room had been clean as a whistle. "The carpeting under my feet," he signaled from the lobby, "is springy and new. I think it must be some miracle fiber. It's blue. You know what I mean by *blue?*" And so on.

When he got to the auditorium itself, the house lights were on. Nobody was there but the manager, who was also the ticket-taker and the bouncer and the janitor. He was sweeping filth from between the seats. He was a middle-aged white man. "No more fun tonight, grandfather," he said to Trout. "Time to go home."

Trout didn't protest. Neither did he leave immediately. He examined a green enameled steel box in the back of the auditorium. It contained the projector and the sound system and the films. There was a wire that led from the box to a plug in the wall. There was a hole in the front of the box. That was how the pictures got out. On the side of the box was a simple switch. It looked like this:

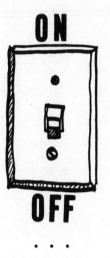

. . .

It intrigued Trout to know that he had only to flick the switch, and the people would start fucking and sucking again.

"Good night, Grandfather," said the manager pointedly.

Trout took his leave of the machine reluctantly. He said this about it to the manager: "It fills such a *need,* this machine, and it's so easy to operate."

. . .

As Trout departed, he sent this telepathic message to the Creator of the Universe, serving as His eyes and ears and conscience: "Am headed for Forty-second Street now. How much do you already know about Forty-second Street?"

8

TROUT WANDERED out onto the sidewalk of Forty-second Street. It was a dangerous place to be. The whole city was dangerous—because of chemicals and the uneven distribution of wealth and so on. A lot of people were like Dwayne: they created chemicals in their own bodies which were bad for their heads. But there were thousands upon thousands of other people in the city who bought bad chemicals and ate them or sniffed them—or injected them into their veins with devices which looked like this:

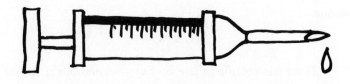

Sometimes they even stuffed bad chemicals up their assholes. Their assholes looked like this:

. . .

People took such awful chances with chemicals and their bodies because they wanted the quality of their lives to improve. They lived in ugly places where there were only ugly things to do. They didn't own doodley-squat, so they couldn't improve their surroundings. So they did their best to make their insides beautiful instead.

The results had been catastrophic so far—suicide, theft, murder, and insanity and so on. But new chemicals were coming onto the market all the time. Twenty feet away from Trout there on Forty-second Street, a fourteen-year-old white boy lay unconscious in the doorway of a pornography store. He had swallowed a half pint of a new type of paint remover which had gone on sale for the first time only the day before. He had also swallowed two pills which were intended to prevent contagious abortion in cattle, which was called *Bang's disease*.

. . .

Trout was petrified there on Forty-second Street. It had given him a life not worth living, but I had also given him an iron will to live. This was a common combination on the planet Earth.

The theater manager came out and locked the door behind him.

And two young black prostitutes materialized from nowhere. They asked Trout and the manager if they would like to have some fun. They were cheerful and unafraid—because of a tube of Norwegian hemorrhoid remedy which they had eaten about half an hour before. The manufacturer had never intended the stuff to be eaten. People were supposed to squirt it up their assholes.

These were country girls. They had grown up in the rural south of the nation, where their ancestors had been used as agricultural machinery. The white farmers down there weren't using machines made out of meat anymore, though, because machines made out of metal were cheaper and more reliable, and required simpler homes.

So the black machines had to get out of there, or starve to death. They came to cities because everyplace else had signs like this on the fences and trees:

• • •

Kilgore Trout once wrote a story called "This Means You." It was set in the Hawaiian Islands, the place where the lucky winners of Dwayne Hoover's contest in Midland City were supposed to go. Every bit of land on the islands was owned by only about forty people, and, in the story, Trout had those people decide to exercise their property rights to the full. They put up *no trespassing* signs on everything.

This created terrible problems for the million other people on the islands. The law of gravity required that they stick somewhere on the surface. Either that, or they could go out into the water and bob offshore.

But then the Federal Government came through with an emergency program. It gave a big balloon full of helium to every man, woman and child who didn't own property.

· · ·

There was a cable with a harness on it dangling from each balloon. With the help of the balloons, Hawaiians could go on inhabiting the islands without always sticking to things other people owned.

· · ·

The prostitutes worked for a pimp now. He was splendid and cruel. He was a god to them. He took their free will away from them, which was perfectly all right. They didn't want it anyway. It was as though they had surrendered themselves to Jesus, for instance, so they could live unselfishly and trustingly—except that they had surrendered to a pimp instead.

Their childhoods were over. They were dying now. Earth was a tinhorn planet as far as they were concerned.

When Trout and the theater manager, two tinhorns, said they didn't want any tinhorn fun, the dying children sauntered off, their feet sticking to the planet, coming unstuck, then sticking again. They disappeared around a corner. Trout, the eyes and ears of the Creator of the Universe, sneezed.

• • •

"God bless you," said the manager. This was a fully automatic response many Americans had to hearing a person sneeze.

"Thank you," said Trout. Thus a temporary friendship was formed.

Trout said he hoped to get safely to a cheap hotel. The manager said he hoped, to get to the subway station on Times Square. So they walked together, encouraged by the echoes of their footsteps from the building façades.

The manager told Trout a little about what the planet looked like to him. It was a place where he had a wife and two kids, he said. They didn't know he ran a theater which showed blue movies. They thought he was doing consulting work as an engineer so late at night. He said that the planet didn't have much use for engineers his age anymore. It had adored them once.

"Hard times," said Trout.

The manager told of being in on the development of a miraculous insulating material, which had been used on rocket ships to the Moon. This was, in fact, the same material which gave the aluminum siding of Dwayne Hoover's dream house in Midland City its miraculous insulating qualities.

The manager reminded Trout of what the first man to set foot on the Moon had said: "One small step for man, one great leap for mankind."

"Thrilling words," said Trout. He looked over his shoulder, perceived that they were being followed by a white Oldsmobile *Toronado* with a black vinyl roof. This four hundred horsepower, front-wheel drive vehicle was burbling along at about three miles an hour, ten feet behind them and close to the curb.

That was the last thing Trout remembered—seeing the Oldsmobile back there.

• • •

The next thing he knew, he was on his hands and knees on a handball court underneath the Queensboro Bridge at Fifty-ninth Street, with the East River nearby. His trousers and underpants were around his ankles. His money was gone. His parcels were scattered around him—the tuxedo, the new shirt, the books. Blood seeped from one ear.

The police caught him in the act of pulling up his trousers. They dazzled him with a spotlight as he leaned against the backboard of the handball court and fumbled foolishly with his belt and the buttons on his fly. The police supposed that they had caught him committing some public nuisance, had caught him working with an old man's limited palette of excrement and alcohol.

He wasn't quite penniless. There was a ten-dollar bill in the watch pocket of his pants.

• • •

It was determined at a hospital that Trout was not seriously hurt. He was taken to a police station, where he was questioned. All he could say was that he had been kidnapped by pure evil in a white Oldsmobile. The police wanted to know how many people were in the car, their ages, their sexes, the colors of their skins, their manners of speech.

"For all I know, they may not even have been Earthlings," said Trout. "For all I know, that car may have been occupied by an intelligent gas from Pluto."

• • •

Trout said this so innocently, but his comment turned out to be the first germ in an epidemic of mind-poisoning. Here is how the disease was spread: a reporter wrote a story for the *New York Post* the next day, and he led off with the quotation from Trout.

The story appeared under this headline:

PLUTO BANDITS
KIDNAP PAIR

Trout's name was given as Kilmer Trotter, incidentally, address unknown. His age was given as eighty-two.

Other papers copied the story, rewrote it some. They all hung on to the joke about Pluto, spoke knowingly of *The Pluto Gang*. And reporters asked police for any new information on *The Pluto Gang,* so police went looking for information on *The Pluto Gang*.

• • •

So New Yorkers, who had so many nameless terrors, were easily taught to fear something seemingly specific—*The Pluto Gang*. They bought new locks for their doors and gratings for their windows, to keep out *The Pluto Gang*. They stopped going to theaters at night, for fear of *The Pluto Gang*.

Foreign newspapers spread the terror, ran articles on how persons thinking of visiting New York might keep to a certain few streets in Manhattan and stand a fair chance of avoiding *The Pluto Gang*.

• • •

In one of New York City's many ghettos for dark-skinned people, a group of Puerto Rican boys gathered together in the basement of an abandoned building. They were small, but they were numerous and volatile. They wished to become frightening, in order to defend themselves and their friends and families, something the police wouldn't do. They also wanted to drive the drug peddlers out of the neighborhood, and to get enough publicity, which was very important, to catch the attention of the Government, so that the Government would do a better job of picking up the garbage and so on.

One of them, José Mendoza, was a fairly good painter. So he painted the emblem of their new gang on the backs of the members' jackets. This was it:

9

WHILE **K**ILGORE **T**ROUT was inadvertently poisoning the collective mind of New York City, Dwayne Hoover, the demented Pontiac dealer, was coming down from the roof of his own Holiday Inn in the Middle West.

Dwayne went into the carpeted lobby of the place not long before sunrise, to ask for a room. As queer as the hour was, there was a man ahead of him, and a black one at that. This was Cyprian Ukwende, the Indaro, the physician from Nigeria, who was staying at the Inn until he could find a suitable apartment.

Dwayne awaited his turn humbly. He had forgotten that he was a co-owner of the Inn. As for staying at a place where black men stayed, Dwayne was philosophical. He experienced a sort of bittersweet happiness as he told himself, "Times change. Times change."

· · ·

The night clerk was new. He did not know Dwayne. He had Dwayne fill out a registration in full. Dwayne, for his part, apologized for not knowing what the number of his license plate was. He felt guilty about that, even though he knew he had done nothing he should feel guilty about.

He was elated when the clerk let him have a room key. He had passed the test. And he adored his room. It was so new and cool and clean. It was so *neutral!* It was the brother of thousands upon thousands of rooms in Holiday Inns all over the world.

Dwayne Hoover might be confused as to what his life was all about, or what he should do with it next. But this much he has done correctly: He had delivered himself to an irreproachable container for a human being.

It awaited anybody. It awaited Dwayne.

Around the toilet seat was a band of paper like this, which he would have to remove before he used the toilet:

This loop of paper guaranteed Dwayne that he need have no fear that corkscrew-shaped little animals would crawl up his asshole and eat up his wiring. That was one less worry for Dwayne.

• • •

There was a sign hanging on the inside doorknob, which Dwayne now hung on the outside doorknob. It looked like this:

Dwayne pulled open his floor-to-ceiling draperies for a moment. He saw the sign which announced the presence of the Inn to weary travelers on the Interstate. Here is what it looked like:

He closed his draperies. He adjusted the heating and ventilating system. He slept like a lamb.

A lamb was a young animal which was legendary for sleeping well on the planet Earth. It looked like this:

10

KILGORE **T**ROUT was released by the Police Department of the City of New York like a weightless thing—at two hours before dawn on the day after Veterans' Day. He crossed the island of Manhattan from east to west in the company of Kleenex tissues and newspapers and soot.

He got a ride in a truck. It was hauling seventy-eight thousand pounds of Spanish olives. It picked him up at the mouth of the Lincoln Tunnel, which was named in honor of a man who had had the courage and imagination to make human slavery against the law in the United States of America. This was a recent innovation.

The slaves were simply turned loose without any property. They were easily recognizable. They were black. They were suddenly free to go exploring.

• • •

The driver, who was white, told Trout that he would have to lie on the floor of the cab until they reached open country, since it was against the law for him to pick up hitchhikers.

. . .

It was still dark when he told Trout he could sit up. They were crossing the poisoned marshes and meadows of New Jersey. The truck was a General Motors Astro-95 Diesel tractor, hooked up to a trailer forty feet long. It was so enormous that it made Trout feel that his head was about the size of a piece of bee-bee shot.

The driver said he used to be a hunter and a fisherman, long ago. It broke his heart when he imagined what the marshes and meadows had been like only a hundred years before. "And when you think of the shit that most of these factories make—wash day products, catfood, pop—"

. . .

He had a point. The planet was being destroyed by manufacturing processes, and what was being manufactured was lousy, by and large.

Then Trout made a good point, too. "Well," he said, "I used to be a conservationist. I used to weep and wail about people shooting bald eagles with automatic shotguns from helicopters and all that, but I gave it up. There's a river in Cleveland which is so polluted that it catches fire about once a year. That used to make me sick, but I laugh about it now. When some tanker accidently dumps its load in the ocean, and kills millions of birds and billions of fish, I say, 'More power to Standard Oil,' or whoever it was that dumped it." Trout raised his arms in celebration. " 'Up your ass with Mobil gas,' " he said.

The driver was upset by this. "You're kidding," he said.

"I realized," said Trout, "that God wasn't any conservationist, so for anybody else to be one was sacrilegious and a waste of time. You ever see one of His volcanoes or tornadoes or tidal waves? Anybody ever tell you about the Ice Ages he arranges for every half-million years? How about Dutch Elm disease? There's a nice conservation measure for you. That's God, not man. Just about the time we got our rivers cleaned up, he'd probably have the whole galaxy go up like a celluloid collar. That's what the Star of Bethlehem was, you know."

"What *was* the Star of Bethlehem?" said the driver.

"A whole galaxy going up like a celluloid collar," said Trout.

• • •

The driver was impressed. "Come to think about it," he said, "I don't think there's anything about conservation anywhere in the Bible."

"Unless you want to count the story about the Flood," said Trout.

• • •

They rode in silence for a while, and then the driver made another good point. He said he knew that his truck was turning the atmosphere into poison gas, and that the planet was being turned into pavement so his truck could go anywhere. "So I'm committing suicide," he said.

"Don't worry about it," said Trout.

"My brother is even worse," the driver went on. "He works in a factory that makes chemicals for killing plants and trees in Viet Nam." Viet Nam was a country where America

87

was trying to make people stop being communists by dropping things on them from airplanes. The chemicals he mentioned were intended to kill all the foliage, so it would be harder for communists to hide from airplanes.

"Don't worry about it," said Trout.

"In the long run, *he's* committing suicide," said the driver. "Seems like the only kind of job an American can get these days is committing suicide in some way."

"Good point," said Trout.

• • •

"I can't tell if you're serious or not," said the driver.

"I won't know myself until I find out whether *life* is serious or not," said Trout. "It's *dangerous,* I know, and it can hurt a lot. That doesn't necessarily mean it's *serious,* too."

• • •

After Trout became famous, of course, one of the biggest mysteries about him was whether he was kidding or not. He told one persistent questioner that he always crossed his fingers when he was kidding.

"And please note," he went on, "that when I gave you that priceless piece of information, my fingers were crossed."

And so on.

He was a pain in the neck in a lot of ways. The truck driver got sick of him after an hour or two. Trout used the silence to make up an anticonservation story he called "Gilgongo!"

"Gilgongo!" was about a planet which was unpleasant because there was too much creation going on.

The story began with a big party in honor of a man who had wiped out an entire species of darling little panda bears.

He had devoted his life to this. Special plates were made for the party, and the guests got to take them home as souvenirs. There was a picture of a little bear on each one, and the date of the party. Underneath the picture was the word:

GILGONGO!

In the language of the planet, that meant "Extinct!"

. . .

People were glad that the bears were *gilgongo,* because there were too many species on the planet already, and new ones were coming into being almost every hour. There was no way anybody could prepare for the bewildering diversity of creatures and plants he was likely to encounter.

The people were doing their best to cut down on the number of species, so that life could be more predictable. But Nature was too creative for them. All life on the planet was suffocated at last by a living blanket one hundred feet thick. The blanket was composed of passenger pigeons and eagles and Bermuda Erns and whooping cranes.

. . .

"At least it's olives," the driver said.

"What?" said Trout.

"Lots worse things we could be hauling than olives."

"Right," said Trout. He had forgotten that the main thing they were doing was moving seventy-eight thousand pounds of olives to Tulsa, Oklahoma.

. . .

The driver talked about politics some.

Trout couldn't tell one politician from another one. They were all formlessly enthusiastic chimpanzees to him. He wrote a story one time about an optimistic chimpanzee who became President of the United States. He called it "Hail to the Chief."

The chimpanzee wore a little blue blazer with brass buttons, and with the seal of the President of the United States sewed to the breast pocket. It looked like this:

Everywhere he went, bands would play "Hail to the Chief." The chimpanzee loved it. He would bounce up and down.

• • •

They stopped at a diner. Here is what the sign in front of the diner said:

So they ate.

Trout spotted an idiot who was eating, too. The idiot was a white male adult—in the care of a white female nurse. The idiot couldn't talk much, and he had a lot of trouble feeding himself. The nurse put a bib around his neck.

But he certainly had a wonderful appetite. Trout watched him shovel waffles and pork sausage into his mouth, watched him guzzle orange juice and milk. Trout marveled at what a big animal the idiot was. The idiot's happiness was fascinating, too, as he stoked himself with calories which would get him through yet another day.

Trout said this to himself: "Stoking up for another day."

• • •

"Excuse me," said the truck driver to Trout, "I've got to take a leak."

"Back where I come from," said Trout, "that means you're going to steal a mirror. We call mirrors *leaks*."

"I never heard that before," said the driver. He repeated

the word: "Leaks." He pointed to a mirror on a cigarette machine. "You call that a *leak*?"

"Doesn't it look like a leak to you?" said Trout.

"No," said the driver. "Where did you say you were from?"

"I was born in Bermuda," said Trout.

About a week later, the driver would tell his wife that mirrors were called *leaks* in Bermuda, and she would tell her friends.

. . .

When Trout followed the driver back to the truck, he took his first good look at their form of transportation from a distance, saw it whole. There was a message written on the side of it in bright orange letters which were eight feet high. This was it:

Trout wondered what a child who was just learning to read would make of a message like that. The child would suppose that the message was terrifically important, since somebody had gone to the trouble of writing it in letters so big.

And then, pretending to be a child by the roadside, he read the message on the side of another truck. This was it:

11

DWAYNE HOOVER slept until ten at the new Holiday Inn. He was much refreshed. He had a Number Five Breakfast in the popular restaurant of the Inn, which was the *Tally-Ho Room*. The drapes were drawn at night. They were wide open now. They let the sunshine in.

At the next table, also alone, was Cyprian Ukwende, the Indaro, the Nigerian. He was reading the classified ads in the Midland City *Bugle-Observer*. He needed a cheap place to live. The Midland County General Hospital was footing his bills at the Inn while he looked around, and they were getting restless about that.

He needed a woman, too, or a bunch of women who would fuck him hundreds of times a week, because he was so full of lust and jism all the time. And he ached to be with his Indaro relatives. Back home, he had six hundred relatives he knew by name.

Ukwende's face was impassive as he ordered the Number Three Breakfast with whole-wheat toast. Behind his mask was a young man in the terminal stages of nostalgia and lover's nuts.

. . .

Dwayne Hoover, six feet away, gazed out at the busy, sunny Interstate Highway. He knew where he was. There was a familiar moat between the parking lot of the Inn and the Interstate, a concrete trough which the engineers had built to contain Sugar Creek. Next came a familiar resilient steel barrier which prevented cars and trucks from tumbling into Sugar Creek. Next came the three familiar west-bound lanes, and then the familiar grassy median divider. After that came the three familiar east-bound lanes, and then another familiar steel barrier. After that came the familiar Will Fairchild Memorial Airport—and then the familiar farmlands beyond.

. . .

It was certainly flat out there—flat city, flat township, flat county, flat state. When Dwayne was a little boy, he had supposed that almost everybody lived in places that were treeless and flat. He imagined that oceans and mountains and forests were mainly sequestered in state and national parks. In the third grade, little Dwayne scrawled an essay which argued in favor of creating a national park at a bend in Sugar Creek, the only significant surface water within eight miles of Midland City.

Dwayne said the name of that familiar surface water to himself now, silently: "Sugar Creek."

. . .

Sugar Creek was only two inches deep and fifty yards wide at the bend, where little Dwayne thought the park should be. Now they had put the Mildred Barry Memorial Center for the Arts there instead. It was beautiful.

Dwayne fiddled with his lapel for a moment, felt a badge pinned there. He unpinned it, having no recollection of what it said. It was a boost for the Arts Festival, which would begin that evening. All over town people were wearing badges like Dwayne's. Here is what the badges said:

• • •

Sugar Creek flooded now and then. Dwayne remembered about that. In a land so flat, flooding was a queerly pretty thing for water to do. Sugar Creek brimmed over silently, formed a vast mirror in which children might safely play.

The mirror showed the citizens the shape of the valley they lived in, demonstrated that they were hill people who inhabited slopes rising one inch for every mile that separated them from Sugar Creek.

Dwayne silently said the name of the water again: "Sugar Creek."

•   •   •

Dwayne finished his breakfast, and he dared to suppose that he was no longer mentally diseased, that he had been cured by a simple change of residence, by a good night's sleep.

His bad chemicals let him cross the lobby and then the cocktail lounge, which wasn't open yet, without experiencing anything strange. But when he stepped out of the side door of the cocktail lounge, and onto the asphalt prairie which surrounded both his Inn and his Pontiac agency, he discovered that someone had turned the asphalt into a sort of trampoline.

It sank beneath Dwayne's weight. It dropped Dwayne to well below street level, then slowly brought him only partway up again. He was in a shallow, rubbery dimple. Dwayne took another step in the direction of his automobile agency. He sank down again, came up again, and stood in a brand new dimple.

He gawked around for witnesses. There was only one. Cyprian Ukwende stood on the rim of the dimple, not sinking in. This was all Ukwende had to say, even though Dwayne's situation was extraordinary:

"Nice day."

•   •   •

Dwayne progressed from dimple to dimple.

He blooped across the used car lot now.

He stopped in a dimple, looked up at another young black man. This one was polishing a maroon 1970 Buick *Skylark* convertible with a rag. The man wasn't dressed for that sort of work. He wore a cheap blue suit and a white shirt and a black necktie. Also: he wasn't merely polishing the car—he was *burnishing* it.

The young man did some more burnishing. Then he smiled at Dwayne blindingly, then he burnished the car again.

Here was the explanation: this young black man had just been paroled from the Adult Correctional Institution at Shepherdstown. He needed work right away, or he would starve to death. So he was showing Dwayne how hard a worker he was.

He had been in orphanages and youth shelters and prisons of one sort or another in the Midland City area since he was nine years old. He was now twenty-six.

• • •

He was free at last!

• • •

Dwayne thought the young man was an hallucination.

• • •

The young man went back to burnishing the automobile. His life was not worth living. He had a feeble will to survive. He thought the planet was terrible, that he never should have been sent there. Some mistake had been made. He had no friends or relatives. He was put in cages all the time.

He had a name for a better world, and he often saw it in dreams. Its name was a secret. He would have been ridiculed, if he had said its name out loud. It was such a *childish* name.

The young black jailbird could see the name any time he wanted to, written in lights on the inside of his skull. This is what it looked like:

. . .

He had a photograph of Dwayne in his wallet. He used to have photographs of Dwayne on the walls of his cell at Shepherdstown. They were easy to get, because Dwayne's smiling face, with his motto underneath, was a part of every ad he ran in the *Bugle-Observer*. The picture was changed every six months. The motto hadn't varied in twenty-five years.

Here was the motto:

ASK ANYBODY—
YOU CAN TRUST
DWAYNE.

The young ex-convict smiled yet again at Dwayne. His teeth were in perfect repair. The dental program at Shepherdstown was excellent. So was the food.

"Good morning, sir," said the young man to Dwayne.

He was dismayingly innocent. There was so much he had to learn. He didn't know anything about women, for instance. Francine Pefko was the first woman he had spoken to in eleven years.

"Good morning," said Dwayne. He said it softly, so his voice wouldn't carry very far, in case he was conversing with an hallucination.

"Sir—I have read your ads in the newspapers with great interest, and I have found pleasure in your radio advertising, too," the parolee said. During the last year in prison, he had been obsessed by one idea: that he would work for Dwayne someday, and live happily ever after. It would be like Fairyland.

Dwayne made no reply to this, so the young man went on: "I am a very hard worker, sir, as you can see. I hear nothing but good things about you. I think the good Lord meant for me to work for you."

"Oh?" said Dwayne.

"Our names are so close," said the young man, "it's the good Lord telling us *both* what to do."

Dwayne Hoover didn't ask him what his name was, but the young man told him anyway, radiantly: "My name, sir, is Wayne Hoobler."

All around Midland City, Hoobler was a common Nigger name.

• • •

Dwayne Hoover broke Wayne Hoobler's heart by shaking his head vaguely, then walking away.

• • •

Dwayne entered his showroom. The ground wasn't blooping underneath him anymore, but now he saw something else for which there could be no explanation: A palm tree was growing out of the showroom floor. Dwayne's bad chemicals made him forget all about Hawaiian Week. Actually, Dwayne had designed the palm tree himself. It was a sawed-off telephone pole—swaddled in burlap. It had real coconuts nailed to the top of it. Sheets of green plastic had been cut to resemble leaves.

The tree so bewildered Dwayne that he almost swooned. Then he looked around and saw pineapples and ukuleles scattered everywhere.

And then he saw the most unbelievable thing of all: His sales manager, Harry LeSabre, came toward him leeringly, wearing a lettuce-green leotard, straw sandals, a grass skirt, and a pink T-shirt which looked like this:

• • •

Harry and his wife had spent all weekend arguing about whether or not Dwayne suspected that Harry was a transvestite. They concluded that Dwayne had no reason to suspect it. Harry never talked about women's clothes to Dwayne. He had never entered a transvestite beauty contest or done what a lot of transvestites in Midland City did, which was join a big transvestite club over in Cincinnati. He never went into the city's transvestite bar, which was *Ye Old Rathskeller,* in the basement of the Fairchild Hotel. He had never exchanged Polaroid pictures with any other transvestites, had never subscribed to a transvestite magazine.

Harry and his wife concluded that Dwayne had meant nothing more than what he said, that Harry had better put on some wild clothes for Hawaiian Week, or Dwayne would can him.

So here was the new Harry now, rosy with fear and excitement. He felt uninhibited and beautiful and lovable and suddenly free.

He greeted Dwayne with the Hawaiian word which meant both *hello* and *goodbye.* "Aloha," he said.

12

KILGORE TROUT was far away, but he was steadily closing the distance between himself and Dwayne. He was still in the truck named *Pyramid*. It was crossing a bridge named in honor of the poet Walt Whitman. The bridge was veiled in smoke. The truck was about to become a part of Philadelphia now. A sign at the foot of the bridge said this:

YOU ARE NOW ENTERING
THE CITY OF
BROTHERLY LOVE

· · ·

As a younger man, Trout would have sneered at the sign about brotherhood—posted on the rim of a bomb crater, as anyone could see. But his head no longer sheltered ideas of how things could be and should be on the planet, as opposed to how they really were. There was only one way for the Earth to be, he thought: the way it was.

Everything was necessary. He saw an old white woman fishing through a garbage can. That was necessary. He saw a bathtub toy, a little rubber duck, lying on its side on the grating over a storm sewer. It *had* to be there.

And so on.

• • •

The driver mentioned that the day before had been Veterans' Day.

"Um," said Trout.

"You a veteran?" said the driver.

"No," said Trout. "Are you?"

"No," said the driver.

Neither one of them was a veteran.

• • •

The driver got onto the subject of friends. He said it was hard for him to maintain friendships that meant anything because he was on the road most of the time. He joked about the time when he used to talk about his "best friends." He guessed people stopped talking about best friends after they got out of junior high school.

He suggested that Trout, since Trout was in the combination aluminum storm window and screen business, had opportunities to build many lasting friendships in the course of his work. "I mean," he said, "you get men working together day after day, putting up those windows, they get to know each other pretty well."

"I work alone," said Trout.

The driver was disappointed. "I assumed it would take two men to do the job."

"Just one," said Trout. "A weak little kid could do it without any help."

The driver wanted Trout to have a rich social life so that he could enjoy it vicariously. "All the same," he insisted, "you've got buddies you see after work. You have a few beers. You play some cards. You have some laughs."

Trout shrugged.

"You walk down the same streets every day," the driver told him. "You know a lot of people, and they know you, because it's the same streets for you, day after day. You say, 'Hello,' and they say 'Hello,' back. You call them by name. They call you by name. If you're in a real jam, they'll help you, because you're one of 'em. You *belong*. They see you every day."

Trout didn't want to argue about it.

• • •

Trout had forgotten the driver's name.

Trout had a mental defect which I, too, used to suffer from. He couldn't remember what different people in his life looked like—unless their bodies or faces were strikingly unusual.

When he lived on Cape Cod, for instance, the only person he could greet warmly and by name was Alfy Bearse, who was a one-armed albino. "Hot enough for you, Alfy?" he would say. "Where you been keeping yourself, Alfy?" he'd say. "You're a sight for sore eyes, Alfy," he'd say.

And so on.

• • •

Now that Trout lived in Cohoes, the only person he called by name was a red-headed Cockney midget, Durling Heath. He worked in a shoe repair shop. Heath had an executive-type nameplate on his workbench, in case anybody wished to address him by name. The nameplate looked like this:

Trout would drop into the shop from time to time, and say such things as, "Who's gonna win the World Series this year, Durling?" and "You have any idea what all the sirens were blowing about last night, Durling?" and, "You're looking good today, Durling—where'd you get that shirt?" And so on.

Trout wondered now if his friendship with Heath was over. The last time Trout had been in the shoe repair place, saying this and that to Durling, the midget had unexpectedly screamed at him.

This is what he had screamed in his Cockney accent: "Stop bloody *hounding* me!"

• • •

The Governor of New York, Nelson Rockefeller, shook Trout's hand in a Cohoes grocery story one time. Trout had no idea who he was. As a science-fiction writer, he should have been flabbergasted to come so close to such a man.

Rockefeller wasn't merely Governor. Because of the peculiar laws in that part of the planet, Rockefeller was allowed to own vast areas of Earth's surface, and the petroleum and other valuable minerals underneath the surface, as well. He owned or controlled more of the planet than many nations. This had been his destiny since infancy. He had been *born* into that cockamamie proprietorship.

"How's it going, fella?" Governor Rockefeller asked him.

"About the same," said Kilgore Trout.

• • •

After insisting that Trout had a rich social life, the driver pretended, again for his own gratification, that Trout had begged to know what the sex life of a transcontinental truck driver was like. Trout had begged no such thing.

"You want to know how truck drivers make out with women, right?" the driver said. "You have this idea that every driver you see is fucking up a storm from coast to coast, right?"

Trout shrugged.

The truck driver became embittered by Trout, scolded him for being so salaciously misinformed. "Let me tell you, Kilgore—" he hesitated. "That's your name, right?"

"Yes," said Trout. He had forgotten the driver's name a hundred times. Every time Trout looked away from him, Trout forgot not only his name but his face, too.

"Kilgore, God damn it—" the driver said, "if I was to have my rig break down in Cohoes, for instance, and I was to have to stay there for two days while it was worked on, how easy you think it would be for me to get laid while I was there—a stranger, looking the way I do?"

"It would depend on how *determined* you were," said Trout.

The driver sighed. "Yeah, God—" he said, and he despaired for himself, "that's probably the story of my life: not enough determination."

• • •

They talked about aluminum siding as a technique for making old houses look new again. From a distance, these sheets, which never needed painting, looked like freshly painted wood.

The driver wanted to talk about *Perma-Stone,* too, which was a competitive scheme. It involved plastering the sides of old houses with colored cement, so that, from a distance, they looked as though they were made of stone.

"If you're in aluminum storm windows," the driver said to Trout, "you must be in aluminum siding, too." All over the country, the two businesses went hand-in-hand.

"My company sells it," said Trout, "and I've seen a lot of it. I've never actually worked on an installation."

The driver was thinking seriously of buying aluminum siding for his home in Little Rock, and he begged Trout to give him an honest answer to this question: "From what you've seen and heard—the people who get aluminum siding, are they *happy* with what they get?"

"Around Cohoes," said Trout. "I think those were about the only really happy people I ever saw."

• • •

"I know what you mean," said the driver. "One time I saw a whole family standing outside their house. They couldn't believe how nice their house looked after the aluminum siding went on. My question to you, and you can give me an honest answer, on account of we'll never have to do business, you and me: Kilgore, how long will that happiness last?"

"About fifteen years," said Trout. "Our salesmen say you can easily afford to have the job redone with all the money you've saved on paint and heat."

"*Perma-Stone* looks a lot richer, and I suppose it lasts a lot longer, too," said the driver. "On the other hand, it costs a lot more."

"You get what you pay for," said Kilgore Trout.

• • •

The truck driver told Trout about a gas hot-water heater he had bought thirty years ago, and it hadn't given him a speck of trouble in all that time.

"I'll be damned," said Kilgore Trout.

• • •

Trout asked about the truck, and the driver said it was the greatest truck in the world. The tractor alone cost twenty-eight thousand dollars. It was powered by a three hundred and twenty-four horsepower Cummins Diesel engine, which was turbo-charged, so it would function well at high altitudes. It had hydraulic steering, air brakes, a thirteen-speed transmission, and was owned by his brother-in-law.

His brother-in-law, he said, owned twenty-eight trucks, and was President of the Pyramid Trucking Company.

"Why did he name his company *Pyramid*?" asked Trout. "I mean—this thing can go a hundred miles an hour, if it has to. It's fast and useful and unornamental. It's as up-to-date as a rocket ship. I never saw anything that was less like a pyramid than this truck."

• • •

A pyramid was a sort of huge stone tomb which Egyptians had built thousands and thousands of years before. The Egyptians didn't build them anymore. The tombs looked like this, and tourists would come from far away to gaze at them:

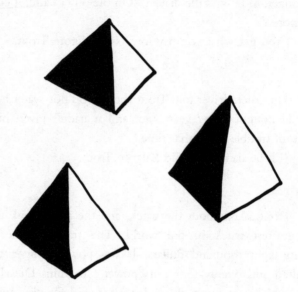

"Why would anybody in the business of highspeed transportation name his business and his trucks after buildings which haven't moved an eighth of an inch since Christ was born?"

The driver's answer was prompt. It was peevish, too, as though he thought Trout was stupid to have to ask a question like that. "He liked the *sound* of it," he said. "Don't you like the *sound* of it?"

Trout nodded in order to keep things friendly. "Yes," he said, "it's a very nice sound."

• • •

Trout sat back and thought about the conversation. He shaped it into a story, which he never got around to writing until he was an old, old man. It was about a planet where the language kept turning into pure music, because the creatures there were so enchanted by sounds. Words became musical notes. Sentences became melodies. They were useless as conveyors of information, because nobody knew or cared what the meanings of words were anymore.

So leaders in government and commerce, in order to function, had to invent new and much uglier vocabularies and sentence structures all the time, which would resist being transmuted to music.

• • •

"You married, Kilgore?" the driver asked.

"Three times," said Trout. It was true. Not only that, but each of his wives had been extraordinarily patient and loving and beautiful. Each had been shriveled by his pessimism.

"Any kids?"

"One," said Trout. Somewhere in the past, tumbling among all the wives and stories lost in the mails was a son named Leo. "He's a man now," said Trout.

• • •

Leo left home forever at the age of fourteen. He lied about his age, and he joined the Marines. He sent a note to

113

his father from boot camp. It said this: "I pity you. You've crawled up your own asshole and died."

That was the last Trout heard from Leo, directly or indirectly, until he was visited by two agents from the Federal Bureau of Investigation. Leo had deserted from his division in Viet Nam, they said. He had committed high treason. He had joined the Viet Cong.

Here was the F.B.I. evaluation of Leo's situation on the planet at that time: "Your boy's in bad trouble," they said.

13

When Dwayne Hoover saw Harry LeSabre, his sales manager, in leaf-green leotards and a grass skirt and all that, he could not believe it. So he made himself not see it. He went into his office, which was also cluttered with ukuleles and pineapples.

Francine Pefko, his secretary, looked normal, except that she had a rope of flowers around her neck and a flower behind one ear. She smiled. This was a war widow with lips like sofa pillows and bright red hair. She adored Dwayne. She adored Hawaiian Week, too.

"Aloha," she said.

• • •

Harry LeSabre, meanwhile, had been destroyed by Dwayne.

When Harry presented himself to Dwayne so ridiculously, every molecule in his body awaited Dwayne's reaction. Each molecule ceased its business for a moment, put some distance between itself and its neighbors. Each

115

molecule waited to learn whether its galaxy, which was called *Harry LeSabre,* would or would not be dissolved.

When Dwayne treated Harry as though he were invisible, Harry thought he had revealed himself as a revolting transvestite, and that he was fired on that account.

Harry closed his eyes. He never wanted to open them again. His heart sent this message to his molecules: "For reasons obvious to us all, this galaxy is *dissolved*!"

• • •

Dwayne didn't know anything about that. He leaned on Francine Pefko's desk. He came close to telling her how sick he was. He warned her: "This is a very tough day, for some reason. So no jokes, no surprises. Keep everything simple. Keep anybody the least bit nutty out of here. No telephone calls."

Francine told Dwayne that the twins were waiting for him in the inner office. "Something bad is happening to the cave, I think," she told him.

Dwayne was grateful for a message that simple and clear. The twins were his younger stepbrothers, Lyle and Kyle Hoover. The cave was Sacred Miracle Cave, a tourist trap just south of Shepherdstown, which Dwayne owned in partnership with Lyle and Kyle. It was the sole source of income for Lyle and Kyle, who lived in identical yellow ranch houses on either side of the gift shop which sheltered the entrance to the cave.

All over the State, nailed to trees and fence posts, were arrow-shaped signs, which pointed in the direction of the cave and said how far away it was—for example:

Before Dwayne entered his inner office, he read one of many comical signs which Francine had put up on the wall in order to amuse people, to remind them of what they so easily forgot: that people didn't have to be serious all the time.

Here was the text of the sign Dwayne read:

> YOU DON'T HAVE TO BE CRAZY
> TO WORK HERE, BUT IT SURE HELPS!

There was a picture of a crazy person to go with the text. This was it:

Francine wore a button on her bosom which showed a creature in a healthier, more enviable frame of mind. This was the button:

• • •

Lyle and Kyle sat side-by-side on the black leather couch in Dwayne Hoover's inner office. They looked so much alike that Dwayne had not been able to tell them apart until 1954, when Lyle got in a fight over a woman at the Roller Derby. After that, Lyle was the one with the broken nose. As babies in crib, Dwayne remembered now, they used to suck each other's thumbs.

• • •

Here is how Dwayne happened to have stepbrothers, incidentally, even though he had been adopted by people who couldn't have children of their own. Their adopting him triggered something to their bodies which made it possible for them to have children after all. This was a common phenomenon. A lot of couples seemed to be programmed that way.

• • •

Dwayne was so glad to see them now—these two little men in overalls and work shoes, each wearing a pork-pie hat. They were familiar, they were *real*. Dwayne closed his door on the chaos outside. "All right—" he said, "what's happened at the cave?"

Ever since Lyle had had his nose broken, the twins agreed that Lyle should do the talking for the two. Kyle hadn't said a thousand words since 1954.

"Them bubbles is halfway up to the *Cathedral* now," said Lyle. "The way they're coming, they'll be up to *Moby Dick* in a week or two."

Dwayne understood him perfectly. The underground stream which passed through the bowels of Sacred Miracle Cave was polluted by some sort of industrial waste which formed bubbles as tough as ping-pong balls. These bubbles were shouldering one another up a passage which led to a big boulder which had been painted white to resemble *Moby Dick, the Great White Whale*. The bubbles would soon engulf *Moby Dick* and invade the *Cathedral of Whispers*, which was the main attraction at the cave. Thousands of people had been married in the *Cathedral of Whispers*—including Dwayne and Lyle and Kyle. Harry LeSabre, too.

• • •

Lyle told Dwayne about an experiment he and Kyle had performed the night before. They had gone into the cave with their identical Browning Automatic Shotguns, and they had opened fire on the advancing wall of bubbles.

"They let loose a stink you wouldn't believe," said Lyle. He said it smelled like athlete's foot. "It drove me and Kyle right out of there. We run the ventilating system for an hour, and then we went back in. The paint was blistered on *Moby*

Dick. He ain't even got eyes anymore." *Moby Dick* used to have long-lashed blue eyes as big as dinner plates.

• • •

"The organ turned black, and the ceiling turned a kind of dirty yellow," said Lyle. "You can't hardly see the *Sacred Miracle* no more."

The organ was the *Pipe Organ of the Gods,* a thicket of stalactites and stalagmites which had grown together in one corner of the *Cathedral.* There was a loudspeaker in back of it, through which music for weddings and funerals was played. It was illuminated by electric lights, which changed colors all the time.

The Sacred Miracle was a cross on the ceiling of the *Cathedral.* It was formed by the intersection of two cracks. "It never *was* real easy to see," said Lyle, speaking of the cross. "I ain't even sure it's there anymore." He asked Dwayne's permission to order a load of cement. He wanted to plug up the passage between the stream and the Cathedral.

"Just forget about *Moby Dick* and *Jesse James* and the slaves and all that," said Lyle, "and save the *Cathedral.*"

Jesse James was a skeleton which Dwayne's stepfather had bought from the estate of a doctor back during the Great Depression. The bones of its right hand mingled with the rusted parts of a .45 caliber revolver. Tourists were told that it had been found that way, that it probably belonged to some railroad robber who had been trapped in the cave by a rock-slide.

As for the slaves: these were plaster statues of black men in a chamber fifty feet down the corridor from *Jesse James.* The statues were removing one another's chains with hammers and hacksaws. Tourists were told that real slaves had at one time used the cave after escaping to freedom across the Ohio River.

· · ·

The story about the slaves was as fake as the one about Jesse James. The cave wasn't discovered until 1937, when a small earthquake opened it up a crack. Dwayne Hoover himself discovered the crack, and then he and his stepfather opened it with crowbars and dynamite. Before that, not even small animals had been in there.

The only connection the cave had with slavery was this: the farm on which it was discovered was started by an ex-slave, Josephus Hoobler. He was freed by his master, and he came north and started the farm. Then he went back and bought his mother and a woman who became his wife.

Their descendants continued to run the farm until the Great Depression, when the Midland County Merchants Bank foreclosed on the mortgage. And then Dwayne's stepfather was hit by an automobile driven by a white man who had bought the farm. In an out-of-court settlement for his injuries, Dwayne's stepfather was given what he called contemptuously ". . . a God damn Nigger farm."

Dwayne remembered the first trip the family took to see it. His father ripped a Nigger sign off the Nigger mailbox, and he threw it into a ditch. Here is what it said:

14

THE TRUCK carrying Kilgore Trout was in West Virginia now. The surface of the State had been demolished by men and machinery and explosives in order to make it yield up its coal. The coal was mostly gone now. It had been turned into heat.

The surface of West Virginia, with its coal and trees and topsoil gone, was rearranging what was left of itself in conformity with the laws of gravity. It was collapsing into all the holes which had been dug into it. Its mountains, which had once found it easy to stand by themselves, were sliding into valleys now.

The demolition of West Virginia had taken place with the approval of the executive, legislative, and judicial branches of the State Government, which drew their power from the people.

Here and there an inhabited dwelling still stood.

. . .

Trout saw a broken guardrail ahead. He gazed into a gully below it, saw a 1968 Cadillac *El Dorado* capsized in a brook. It had Alabama license plates. There were also several old home appliances in the brook—stoves, a washing machine, a couple of refrigerators.

An angel-faced white child, with flaxen hair, stood by the brook. She waved up at Trout. She clasped an eighteen-ounce bottle of *Pepsi-Cola* to her breast.

. . .

Trout asked himself out loud what the people did for amusement, and the driver told him a queer story about a night he spent in West Virginia, in the cab of his truck, near a windowless building which droned monotonously.

"I'd see folks go in, and I'd see folks come out," he said, "but I couldn't figure out what kind of a machine it was that made the drone. The building was a cheap old frame thing set up on cement blocks, and it was out in the middle of nowhere. Cars came and went, and the folks sure seemed to like whatever was doing the droning," he said.

So he had a look inside. "It was full of folks on roller-skates," he said. "They went around and around. Nobody smiled. They just went around and around."

. . .

He told Trout about people he'd heard of in the area who grabbed live copperheads and rattlesnakes during church services, to show how much they believed that Jesus would protect them.

"Takes all kinds of people to make up a world," said Trout.

. . .

Trout marveled at how recently white men had arrived in West Virginia, and how quickly they had demolished it— for heat.

Now the heat was all gone, too—into outer space, Trout supposed. It had boiled water, and the steam had made steel windmills whiz around and around. The windmills had made rotors in generators whiz around and around. America was jazzed with electricity for a while. Coal had also powered old-fashioned steamboats and choo-choo trains.

• • •

Choo-choo trains and steamboats and factories had whistles which were blown by steam when Dwayne Hoover and Kilgore Trout and I were boys—when our fathers were boys, when our grandfathers were boys. The whistles looked like this:

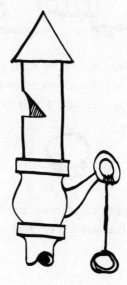

Steam from water boiled by burning coal was sent raging through the whistles, which made harshly beautiful laments, as though they were the voice boxes of mating or dying dinosaurs—cries such as *woooooooo-uh, wooooo-uh,* and *torrrrrrrrrrrrrrr-rrrrrrrrrrrrrrrrrnnnnnnnnnnnnn,* and so on.

. . .

A dinosaur was a reptile as big as a choo-choo train. It looked like this:

It had two brains, one for its front end and one for its rear end. It was extinct. Both brains combined were smaller than a pea. A pea was a legume which looked like this:

Coal was a highly compressed mixture of rotten trees and flowers and bushes and grasses and so on, and dinosaur excrement.

. . .

Kilgore Trout thought about the cries of steam whistles he had known, and about the destruction of West Virginia, which made their songs possible. He supposed that the heart-rending cries had fled into outer space, along with the heat. He was mistaken.

Like most science-fiction writers, Trout knew almost nothing about science, was bored stiff by technical details. But no cry from a whistle had got very far from Earth for this reason: sound could only travel in an atmosphere, and the atmosphere of Earth relative to the planet wasn't even as thick as the skin of an apple. Beyond that lay an all-but-perfect vacuum.

An apple was a popular fruit which looked like this:

• • •

The driver was a big eater. He pulled into a MacDonald's Hamburger establishment. There were many different chains of hamburger establishments in the country. *MacDon-*

ald's was one. *Burger Chef* was another. Dwayne Hoover, as has already been said, owned franchises for several *Burger Chefs*.

• • •

A hamburger was made out of an animal which looked like this:

The animal was killed and ground up into little bits, then shaped into patties and fried, and put between two pieces of bread. The finished product looked like this:

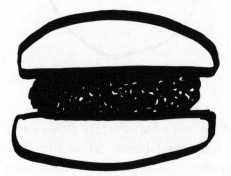

. . .

And Trout, who had so little money left, ordered a cup of coffee. He asked an old, old man on a stool next to him at the table if he had worked in the coal mines.

The old man said this: "From the time I was ten till I was sixty-two."

"You glad to be out of 'em?" said Trout.

"Oh, God," said the man, "you never get out of 'em— even when you sleep. I *dream* mines."

Trout asked him what it had felt like to work for an industry whose business was to destroy the countryside, and the old man said he was usually too tired to care.

. . .

"Don't matter if you care," the old miner said, "if you don't own what you care about." He pointed out that the mineral rights to the entire county in which they sat were owned by the Rosewater Coal and Iron Company, which had acquired these rights soon after the end of the Civil War. "The law says," he went on, "when a man owns something under the ground and he wants to get at it, you got to let him tear up anything between the surface and what he owns."

Trout did not make the connection between the Rosewater Coal and Iron Company and Eliot Rosewater, his only fan. He still thought Eliot Rosewater was a teenager.

The truth was that Rosewater's ancestors had been among the principal destroyers of the surface and the people of West Virginia.

. . .

"It don't seem right, though," the old miner said to Trout, "that a man can own what's underneath another man's farm or woods or house. And any time the man wants to get what's underneath all that, he's got a right to wreck what's on top to get at it. The rights of the people on top of the ground don't amount to nothing compared to the rights of the man who owns what's underneath."

He remembered out loud when he and other miners used to try to force the Rosewater Coal and Iron Company to treat them like human beings. They would fight small wars with the company's private police and the State Police and the National Guard.

"I never saw a Rosewater," he said, "but Rosewater always won. I walked on Rosewater. I dug holes for Rosewater in Rosewater. I lived in Rosewater houses. I ate Rosewater food. I'd fight Rosewater, whatever Rosewater is, and Rosewater would beat me and leave me for dead. You ask people around here and they'll tell you: this whole world is Rosewater as far as *they're* concerned."

• • •

The driver knew Trout was bound for Midland City. He didn't know Trout was a writer on his way to an arts festival. Trout understood that honest working people had no use for the arts.

"Why would anybody in his right mind go to Midland City?" the driver wanted to know. They were riding along again.

"My sister is sick," said Trout.

"Midland City is the asshole of the Universe," said the driver.

"I've often wondered where the asshole was," said Trout.

"If it isn't in Midland City," said the driver, "it's in Libertyville, Georgia. You ever see Libertyville?"

"No," said Trout.

"I was arrested for speeding down there. They had a speed trap, where you all of a sudden had to go from fifty down to fifteen miles an hour. It made me mad. I had some words with the policeman, and he put me in jail.

"The main industry there was pulping up old newspapers and magazines and books, and making new paper out of 'em," said the driver. "Trucks and trains were bringing in hundreds of tons of unwanted printed material every day."

"Um," said Trout.

"And the unloading process was sloppy, so there were pieces of books and magazines and so on blowing all over town. If you wanted to start a library, you could just go over to the freight yard, and carry away all the books you wanted."

"Um," said Trout. Up ahead was a white man hitchhiking with his pregnant wife and nine children.

"Looks like Gary Cooper, don't he?" said the truck driver of the hitchhiking man.

"Yes, he does," said Trout. Gary Cooper was a movie star.

• • •

"Anyway," said the driver, "they had so many books in Libertyville, they used books for toilet paper in the jail. They got me on a Friday, late in the afternoon, so I couldn't have a hearing in court until Monday. So I sat there in the calaboose for two days, with nothing to do but read my toilet paper. I can still remember one of the stories I read."

"Um," said Trout.

"That was the *last* story I ever read," said the driver. "My God—that must be all of fifteen years ago. The story was about another planet. It was a crazy story. They had museums full of paintings all over the place, and the government used a kind of roulette wheel to decide what to put in the museums, and what to throw out."

Kilgore Trout was suddenly woozy with *déjà vu*. The truck driver was reminding him of the premise of a book he hadn't thought about for years. The driver's toilet paper in Libertyville, Georgia, had been *The Barring-gaffner of Bagnialto, or This Year's Masterpiece*, by Kilgore Trout.

• • •

The name of the planet where Trout's book took place was *Bagnialto*, and a "Barring-gaffner" there was a government official who spun a wheel of chance once a year. Citizens submitted works of art to the government, and these were given numbers, and then they were assigned cash values according to the Barring-gaffner's spins of the wheel.

The viewpoint of character of the tale was not the Barring-gaffner, but a humble cobbler named Gooz. Gooz lived alone, and he painted a picture of his cat. It was the only picture he had ever painted. He took it to the Barring-gaffner, who numbered it and put it in a warehouse crammed with works of art.

The painting by Gooz had an unprecedented gush of luck on the wheel. It became worth eighteen thousand *lambos,* the equivalent of one billion dollars on Earth. The Barring-gaffner awarded Gooz a check for that amount, most of which was taken back at once by the tax collector. The picture was given a place of honor in the National Gallery, and people lined up for miles for a chance to see a painting worth a billion dollars.

There was also a huge bonfire of all the paintings and statues and books and so on which the wheel had said were worthless. And then it was discovered that the wheel was rigged, and the Barring-gaffner committed suicide.

• • •

It was an amazing coincidence that the truck driver had read a book by Kilgore Trout. Trout had never met a reader before, and his response now was interesting: He did not admit that he was the father of the book.

• • •

The driver pointed out that all the mailboxes in the area had the same last name painted on them.

"There's another one," he said, indicating a mailbox which looked like this:

The truck was passing through the area where Dwayne Hoover's stepparents had come from. They had trekked from West Virginia to Midland City during the First World War, to make big money at the Keedsler Automobile Company, which was manufacturing airplanes and trucks. When they got to Midland City, they had their name changed legally from *Hoobler* to *Hoover,* because there were so many black people in Midland City named Hoobler.

As Dwayne Hoover's stepfather explained to him one time, "It was embarrassing. Everybody up here naturally assumed Hoobler was a *Nigger* name."

15

DWAYNE HOOVER got through lunch all right that day. He remembered now about Hawaiian Week. The ukuleles and so on were no longer mysterious. The pavement between his automobile agency and the new Holiday Inn was no longer a trampoline.

He drove to lunch alone in an air-conditioned demonstrator, a blue Pontiac *Le Mans* with a cream interior, with his radio on. He heard several of his own radio commercials, which drove home the point: "You can always trust Dwayne."

Though his mental health had improved remarkably since breakfast, a new symptom of illness made itself known. It was incipient echolalia. Dwayne found himself wanting to repeat out loud whatever had just been said.

So when the radio told him, "You can always trust Dwayne," he echoed the last word. "Dwayne," he said.

When the radio said there had been a tornado in Texas, Dwayne said this out loud: "Texas."

Then he heard that husbands of women who had been raped during the war between India and Pakistan wouldn't have anything to do with their wives anymore. The women, in the eyes of their husbands, had become *unclean,* said the radio.

"Unclean," said Dwayne.

• • •

As for Wayne Hoobler, the black ex-convict whose only dream was to work for Dwayne Hoover: he had learned to play hide-and-seek with Dwayne's employees. He did not wish to be ordered off the property for hanging around the used cars. So, when an employee came near, Wayne would wander off to the garbage and trash area behind the Holiday Inn, and gravely study the remains of club sandwiches and empty packs of Salem cigarettes and so on in the cans back there, as though he were a health inspector or some such thing.

When the employee went away, Wayne would drift back to the used cars, keeping the boiled eggs of his eyes peeled for the real Dwayne Hoover.

The real Dwayne Hoover, of course, had in effect denied that he was Dwayne. So, when the real Dwayne came out at lunch time, Wayne, who had nobody to talk to but himself, said this to himself: "That ain't Mr. Hoover. Sure *look* like Mr. Hoover, though. Maybe Mr. Hoover sick today." And so on.

• • •

Dwayne had a hamburger and French fries and a Coke at his newest Burger Chef, which was out on Crestview Avenue, across the street from where the new John F. Kennedy High School was going up. John F. Kennedy had never been in Midland City, but he was a President of the United States who was shot to death. Presidents of the country were often shot to death. The assassins were confused by some of the same bad chemicals which troubled Dwayne.

• • •

Dwayne certainly wasn't alone, as far as having bad chemicals inside of him was concerned. He had plenty of company throughout all history. In his own lifetime, for instance, the people in a country called Germany were so full of bad chemicals for a while that they actually built factories whose only purpose was to kill people by the millions. The people were delivered by railroad trains.

When the Germans were full of bad chemicals, their flag looked like this:

Here is what their flag looked like after they got well again:

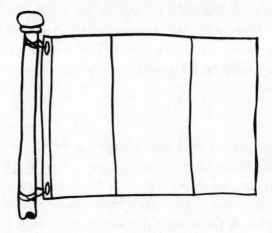

After they got well again, they manufactured a cheap and durable automobile which became popular all over the world, especially among young people. It looked like this:

People called it "the beetle." A real beetle looked like this:

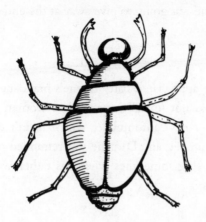

The mechanical beetle was made by Germans. The real beetle was made by the Creator of the Universe.

. . .

Dwayne's waitress at the Burger Chef was a seventeen-year-old white girl named Patty Keene. Her hair was yellow. Her eyes were blue. She was very old for a mammal. Most mammals were senile or dead by the time they were seventeen. But Patty was a sort of mammal which developed very slowly, so the body she rode around in was only now mature.

She was a brand-new adult, who was working in order to pay off the tremendous doctors' and hospital bills her father had run up in the process of dying of cancer of the colon and then cancer of the everything.

This was in a country where everybody was expected to pay his own bills for everything, and one of the most expensive things a person could do was get sick. Patty Keene's father's sickness cost ten times as much as all the trips to Hawaii which Dwayne was going to give away at the end of Hawaiian Week.

• • •

Dwayne appreciated Patty Keene's brand-newness, even though he was not sexually attracted to women that young. She was like a new automobile, which hadn't even had its radio turned on yet, and Dwayne was reminded of a ditty his father would sing sometimes when his father was drunk. It went like this:

> Roses are red,
> And ready for plucking.
> You're sixteen,
> And ready for high school.

Patty Keene was stupid on purpose, which was the case with most women in Midland City. The women all had big minds because they were big animals, but they did not use them much for this reason: unusual ideas could make enemies, and the women, if they were going to achieve any sort of comfort and safety, needed all the friends they could get.

So, in the interests of survival, they trained themselves to be agreeing machines instead of thinking machines. All their minds had to do was to discover what other people were thinking, and then they thought that, too.

• • •

Patty knew who Dwayne was. Dwayne didn't know who Patty was. Patty's heart beat faster when she waited on him—because Dwayne could solve so many of her problems with the money and power he had. He could give her a fine house and new automobiles and nice clothes and a life of leisure, and he could pay all the medical bills—as easily as she had given him his hamburger and his French fries and his Coke.

Dwayne could do for her what the Fairy Godmother did for Cinderella, if he wanted to, and Patty had never been so close to such a magical person before. She was in the presence of the supernatural. And she knew enough about Midland City and herself to understand that she might never be this close to the supernatural ever again.

Patty Keene actually imagined Dwayne's waving a magic wand at her troubles and dreams. It looked like this:

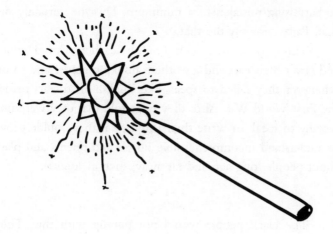

She spoke up bravely, to learn if supernatural assistance was possible in her case. She was willing to do without it, expected to do without it—to work hard all her life, to get not much in return, and to associate with other men and women who were poor and powerless, and in debt. She said this to Dwayne:

"Excuse me for calling you by name, Mr. Hoover, but I can't help knowing who you are, with your picture in all your ads and everything. Besides—everybody else who works here told me who you were. When you came in, they just buzzed and buzzed."

"Buzzed," said Dwayne. This was his echolalia again.

• • •

"I guess that isn't the right word," she said. She was used to apologizing for her use of language. She had been encouraged to do a lot of that in school. Most white people in Midland City were insecure when they spoke, so they kept their sentences short and their words simple, in order to keep embarrassing mistakes to a minimum. Dwayne certainly did that. Patty certainly did that.

This was because their English teachers would wince and cover their ears and give them flunking grades and so on whenever they failed to speak like English aristocrats before the First World War. Also: they were told that they were unworthy to speak or write their language if they couldn't love or understand incomprehensible novels and poems and plays about people long ago and far away, such as *Ivanhoe*.

• • •

The black people would not put up with this. They went on talking English every *which* way. They refused to read books they couldn't understand—on the grounds they couldn't understand them. They would ask such impudent questions as, "Whuffo I want to read no *Tale of Two Cities*? Whuffo?"

• • •

Patty Keene flunked English during the semester when she had to read and appreciate *Ivanhoe,* which was about men in iron suits and the women who loved them. And she was put in a remedial reading class, where they made her read *The Good Earth,* which was about Chinamen.

It was during this same semester that she lost her virginity. She was raped by a white gas-conversion unit installer named Don Breedlove in the parking lot outside the Bannister Memorial Fieldhouse at the County Fairgrounds after the Regional High School Basketball Playoffs. She never reported it to the police. She never reported it to anybody, since her father was dying at the time.

There was enough trouble already.

. . .

The Bannister Memorial Fieldhouse was named in honor of George Hickman Bannister, a seventeen-year-old boy who was killed while playing high school football in 1924. George Hickman Bannister had the largest tombstone in Calvary Cemetery, a sixty-two-foot obelisk with a marble football on top.

The marble football looked like this:

Football was a war game. Two opposing teams fought over the ball while wearing armor made out of leather and cloth and plastic.

George Hickman Bannister was killed while trying to get a hold of the ball on Thanksgiving Day. Thanksgiving Day was a holiday when everybody in the country was expected to express gratitude to the Creator of the Universe, mainly for food.

• • •

George Hickman Bannister's obelisk was paid for by public subscription, with the Chamber of Commerce matching every two dollars raised with a dollar of its own. It was for many years the tallest structure in Midland City. A city ordinance was passed which made it illegal to erect anything taller than that, and it was called *The George Hickman Bannister Law*.

The ordinance was junked later on to allow radio towers to go up.

• • •

The two largest monuments in town, until the new Mildred Barry Memorial Arts Center went up in Sugar Creek, were constructed supposedly so that George Hickman Bannister would never be forgotten. But nobody ever thought about him anymore by the time Dwayne Hoover met Kilgore Trout. There wasn't much to think about him, actually, even at the time of his death, except that he was young.

And he didn't have any relatives in town anymore. There weren't any Bannisters in the phone book, except for *The Bannister,* which was a motion picture theater. Actually, there wouldn't even be a *Bannister Theater* in there after the new phonebooks came out. The Bannister had been turned into a cut-rate furniture store.

George Hickman Bannister's father and mother and sister, Lucy, moved away from town before either the tombstone or the fieldhouse was completed, and they couldn't be located for the dedication ceremonies.

• • •

It was a very restless country, with people tearing around all the time. Every so often, somebody would stop to put up a monument.

There were monuments all over the country. But it was certainly unusual for somebody from the common people to have not one but *two* monuments in his honor, as was the case with George Hickman Bannister.

Technically, though, only the tombstone had been erected specifically for him. The fieldhouse would have gone up anyway. The money was appropriated for the fieldhouse two years before George Hickman Bannister was cut down in his prime. It didn't cost anything extra to name it after him.

• • •

Calvary Cemetery, where George Hickman Bannister was at rest, was named in honor of a hill in Jerusalem, thousands of miles away. Many people believed that the son of the Creator of the Universe had been killed on that hill thousands of years ago.

Dwayne Hoover didn't know whether to believe that or not. Neither did Patty Keene.

. . .

And they certainly weren't worrying about it now. They had other fish to fry. Dwayne was wondering how long his attack of echolalia was likely to last, and Patty Keene had to find out if her brand-newness and prettiness and outgoing personality were worth a lot to a sweet, sort of sexy, middle-aged old Pontiac dealer like Dwayne.

"Anyway," she said, "it certainly is an honor to have you visit us, and those aren't the right words, either, but I hope you know what I mean."

"Mean," said Dwayne.

"Is the food all right?" she said.

"All right," said Dwayne.

"It's what everybody else gets," she said. "We didn't do anything special for you."

"You," said Dwayne.

. . .

It didn't matter much what Dwayne said. It hadn't mattered much for years. It didn't matter much what most people in Midland City said out loud, except when they were talking about money or structures or travel or machinery—or other measurable things. Every person had a clearly defined part to play—as a black person, a female high school drop-out, a Pontiac dealer, a gynecologist, a gas-conversion burner installer. If a person stopped living up to expectations, because of bad chemicals or one thing or another, everybody went on imagining that the person was living up to expectations anyway.

That was the main reason the people in Midland City were so slow to detect insanity in their associates. Their imaginations insisted that nobody changed much from day to day. Their imaginations were flywheels on the ramshackle machinery of the awful truth.

. . .

When Dwayne left Patty Keene and his Burger Chef, when he got into his demonstrator and drove away, Patty Keene was persuaded that she could make him happy with her young body, with her bravery and cheerfulness. She wanted to cry about the lines in his face, and the fact that his wife had eaten Drāno, and that his dog had to fight all the time because it couldn't wag its tail, about the fact that his son was a homosexual. She knew all those things about Dwayne. Everybody knew those things about Dwayne.

She gazed at the tower of radio station WMCY, which Dwayne Hoover owned. It was the tallest structure in Midland City. It was eight times as tall as the tombstone of George Hickman Bannister. It had a red light on top of it—to keep airplanes away.

She thought about all the new and used cars Dwayne owned.

. . .

Earth scientists had just discovered something fascinating about the continent Patty Keene was standing on, incidentally. It was riding on a slab about forty miles thick, and the slab was drifting around on molten glurp. And all the other continents had slabs of their own. When one slab crashed into another one, mountains were made.

. . .

The mountains of West Virginia, for instance, were heaved up when a huge chunk of Africa crashed into North America. And the coal in the state was formed from forests which were buried by the crash.

Patty Keene hadn't heard the big news yet. Neither had Dwayne. Neither had Kilgore Trout. I only found out about it day before yesterday. I was reading a magazine, and I also had the television on. A group of scientists was on television, saying that the theory of floating, crashing, grinding slabs was more than a theory. They could prove it was true now, and that Japan and San Francisco, for instance, were in hideous danger, because that was where some of the most violent crashing and grinding was going on.

They said, too, that ice ages would continue to occur. Mile-thick glaciers would, geologically speaking, continue to go down and up like window blinds.

· · ·

Dwayne Hoover, incidentally, had an unusually large penis, and didn't even know it. The few women he had had anything to do with weren't sufficiently experienced to know whether he was average or not. The world average was five and seven-eighths inches long, and one and one-half inches in diameter when engorged with blood. Dwayne's was seven inches long and two and one-eighth inches in diameter when engorged with blood.

Dwayne's son Bunny had a penis that was exactly average.

Kilgore Trout had a penis seven inches long, but only one and one-quarter inches in diameter.

This was an inch:

148

Harry LeSabre, Dwayne's sales manager, had a penis five inches long and two and one-eighth inches in diameter.

Cyprian Ukwende, the black physician from Nigeria, had a penis six and seven-eighths inches long and one and three-quarters inches in diameter.

Don Breedlove, the gas-conversion unit installer who raped Patty Keene, had a penis five and seven-eighths inches long and one and seven-eighths inches in diameter.

● ● ●

Patty Keene had thirty-four-inch hips, a twenty-six-inch waist, and a thirty-four-inch bosom.

Dwayne's late wife had thirty-six-inch hips, a twenty-eight-inch waist, and a thirty-eight-inch bosom when he married her. She had thirty-nine-inch hips, a thirty-one-inch waist, and a thirty-eight-inch bosom when she ate Drāno.

His mistress and secretary, Francine Pefko, had thirty-seven-inch hips, a thirty-inch waist, and a thirty-nine-inch bosom.

His stepmother at the time of her death had thirty-four-inch hips, a twenty-four-inch waist, and a thirty-three-inch bosom.

● ● ●

So Dwayne went from the Burger Chef to the construction site of the new high school. He was in no hurry to get back to his automobile agency, particularly since he had developed echolalia. Francine was perfectly capable of running the place herself, without any advice from Dwayne. He had trained her well.

So he kicked a little dirt down into the cellar hole. He spat down into it. He stepped into mud. It sucked off his right shoe. He dug the shoe out with his hands, and he wiped it. Then he leaned against an old apple tree while he put the shoe back on. This had all been farmland when Dwayne was a boy. There had been an apple orchard here.

• • •

Dwayne forgot all about Patty Keene, but she certainly hadn't forgotten him. She would get up enough nerve that night to call him on the telephone, but Dwayne wouldn't be home to answer. He would be in a padded cell in the County Hospital by then.

And Dwayne wandered over to admire a tremendous earth-moving machine which had cleared the site and dug the cellar hole. The machine was idle now, caked with mud. Dwayne asked a white workman how many horsepower drove the machine. All the workmen were white.

The workman said this: "I don't know how many horsepower, but I know what we call it."

"What do you call it?" said Dwayne, relieved to find his echolalia was subsiding.

"We call it *The Hundred-Nigger Machine*," said the workman. This had reference to a time when black men had done most of the heavy digging in Midland City.

• • •

The largest human penis in the United States was fourteen inches long and two and a half inches in diameter.

The largest human penis in the world was sixteen and seven-eighths inches long and two and one-quarter inches in diameter.

The blue whale, a sea mammal, had a penis ninety-six inches long and fourteen inches in diameter.

*   *   *

One time Dwayne Hoover got an advertisement through the mail for a penis-extender, made out of rubber. He could slip it over the end of his real penis, according to the ad, and thrill his wife or sweetheart with extra inches. They also wanted to sell him a lifelike rubber vagina for when he was lonesome.

*   *   *

Dwayne went back to work at about two in the afternoon, and he avoided everybody—because of his echolalia. He went into his inner office, and he ransacked his desk drawers for something to read or think about. He came across the brochure which offered him the penis-extender and the rubber vagina for lonesomeness. He had received it two months before. He still hadn't thrown it away.

The brochure also offered him motion pictures such as the ones Kilgore Trout had seen in New York. There were still photographs taken from the movies, and these caused the sex excitation center in Dwayne's brain to send nerve impulses down to an erection center in his spine.

The erection center caused the dorsal vein in his penis to tighten up, so blood could get in all right, but it couldn't get out again. It also relaxed the tiny arteries in his penis, so they filled up the spongy tissue of which Dwayne's penis was mainly composed, so that the penis got hard and stiff—like a plugged-up garden hose.

So Dwayne called Francine Pefko on the telephone, even though she was only eleven feet away. "Francine—?" he said.

"Yes?" she said.

Dwayne fought down his echolalia. "I am going to ask you to do something I have never asked you to do before. Promise me you'll say yes."

"I promise," she said.

"I want you to walk out of here with me this very moment," he said, "and come with me to the Quality Motor Court at Shepherdstown."

• • •

Francine Pefko was willing to go to the Quality Motor Court with Dwayne. It was her duty to go, she thought— especially since Dwayne seemed so depressed and jangled. But she couldn't simply walk away from her desk for the afternoon, since her desk was the nerve center of Dwayne Hoover's Exit Eleven Pontiac Village.

"You ought to have some crazy young teen-ager, who can rush off whenever you want her to," Francine told Dwayne.

"I don't want a crazy teen-ager," said Dwayne. "I want *you*."

"Then you're going to have to be patient," said Francine. She went back to the Service Department, to beg Gloria Browning, the white cashier back there, to man her desk for a little while.

Gloria didn't want to do it. She had had a hysterectomy only a month before, at the age of twenty-five—after a botched abortion at the Ramada Inn down in Green County, on Route 53, across from the entrance to Pioneer Village State Park.

There was a mildly amazing coincidence here: the father of the destroyed fetus was Don Breedlove, the white gas-conversion unit installer who had raped Patty Keene in the parking lot of the Bannister Memorial Fieldhouse.

This was a man with a wife and three kids.

• • •

Francine had a sign on the wall over her desk, which had been given to her as a joke at the automobile agency's Christmas party at the new Holiday Inn the year before.

It spelled out the truth of her situation. This was it:

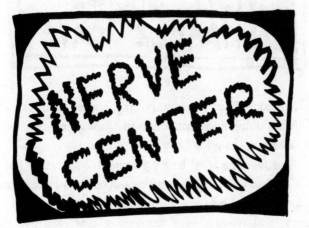

Gloria said she didn't want to man the nerve center. "I don't want to man anything," she said.

• • •

But Gloria took over Francine's desk anyway. "I don't have nerve enough to commit suicide," she said, "so I might as well do anything anybody says—in the service of mankind."

• • •

Dwayne and Francine headed for Shepherdstown in separate cars, so as not to call attention to their love affair. Dwayne was in a demonstrator again. Francine was in her own red GTO. GTO stood for *Gran Turismo Omologato*. She had a sticker on her bumper which said this:

It was certainly loyal of her to put that sticker on her car. She was always doing loyal things like that, always rooting for her man, always rooting for Dwayne.

And Dwayne tried to reciprocate in little ways. For instance, he had been reading articles and books on sexual intercourse recently. There was a sexual revolution going on in the country, and women were demanding that men pay more attention to women's pleasure during sexual intercourse, and not just think of themselves. The key to their pleasure, they said, and scientists backed them up, was the clitoris, a tiny meat cylinder which was right above the hole in women where men were supposed to stick their much larger cylinders.

Men were supposed to pay more attention to the clitoris, and Dwayne had been paying a lot more attention to Francine's, to the point where she said he was paying too much attention to it. This did not surprise him. The things he had read about the clitoris had said that this was a danger—that a man could pay too much attention to it.

So, driving out to the Quality Motor Court that day, Dwayne was hoping that he would pay exactly the right amount of attention to Francine's clitoris.

• • •

Kilgore Trout once wrote a short novel about the importance of the clitoris in love-making. This was in response to a suggestion by his second wife, Darlene, that he could make a fortune with a dirty book. She told him that the hero should understand women so well that he could seduce anyone he wanted. So Trout wrote *The Son of Jimmy Valentine*.

Jimmy Valentine was a famous made-up person in another writer's books, just as Kilgore Trout was a famous made-up person in my books. Jimmy Valentine in the other writer's books sandpapered his fingertips, so they were extrasensitive. He was a safe-cracker. His sense of feel was so delicate that he could open any safe in the world by feeling the tumblers fall.

Kilgore Trout invented a son for Jimmy Valentine, named Ralston Valentine. Ralston Valentine also sandpapered his fingertips. But he wasn't a safe-cracker. Ralston was so good at touching women the way they wanted to be touched, that tens of thousands of them became his willing slaves. They abandoned their husbands or lovers for him, in Trout's story, and Ralston Valentine became President of the United States, thanks to the votes of women.

• • •

Dwayne and Francine made love in the Quality Motor Court. Then they stayed in bed for a while. It was a water bed. Francine had a beautiful body. So did Dwayne. "We never made love in the afternoon before," said Francine.

"I felt so *tense,*" said Dwayne.

"I know," said Francine. "Are you better now?"

"Yes." He was lying on his back. His ankles were crossed. His hands were folded behind his head. His great wang lay across his thigh like a salami. It slumbered now.

"I love you so much," said Francine. She corrected herself. "I know I promised not to say that, but that's a promise I can't help breaking all the time." The thing was: Dwayne had made a pact with her that neither one of them was ever to mention love. Since Dwayne's wife had eaten Drāno, Dwayne never wanted to hear about love ever again. The subject was too painful.

Dwayne snuffled. It was customary for him to communicate by means of snuffles after sexual intercourse. The snuffles all had meanings which were bland: "That's all right . . . forget it . . . who could blame you?" And so on.

"On Judgment Day," said Francine, "when they ask me what bad things I did down here, I'm going to have to tell them, 'Well—there was a promise I made to a man I loved, and I broke it all the time. I promised him never to say I loved him.' "

This generous, voluptuous woman, who had only ninety-six dollars and eleven cents a week in take-home pay, had lost her husband, Robert Pefko, in a war in Viet Nam. He was a career officer in the Army. He had a penis six and one-half inches long and one and seven-eighths inches in diameter.

He was a graduate of West Point, a military academy which turned young men into homicidal maniacs for use in war.

● ● ●

Francine followed Robert from West Point to Parachute School at Fort Bragg, and then to South Korea, where Robert managed a Post Exchange, which was a department store for soldiers, and then to the University of Pennsylvania, where Robert took a Master's Degree in Anthropology, at Army expense, and then back to West Point, where Robert was an Assistant Professor of Social Sciences for three years.

After that, Francine followed Robert to Midland City, where Robert oversaw the manufacture of a new sort of booby trap. A booby trap was an easily hidden explosive device, which blew up when it was accidentally twiddled in some way. One of the virtues of the new type of booby trap was that it could not be smelled by dogs. Various armies at that time were training dogs to sniff out booby traps.

● ● ●

When Robert and Francine were in Midland City, there weren't any other military people around, so they made their first civilian friends. And Francine took a job with Dwayne Hoover, in order to augment her husband's salary and fill her days.

But then Robert was sent to Viet Nam.

Shortly after that, Dwayne's wife ate Drāno and Robert was shipped home in a plastic body bag.

• • •

"I pity men," said Francine, there in the Quality Motor Court. She was sincere. "I wouldn't want to be a man—they take such chances, they work so hard." They were on the second floor of the motel. Their sliding glass doors gave them a view of an iron railing and a concrete terrace outside—and then Route 103, and then the wall and the rooftops of the Adult Correctional Institution beyond that.

"I don't wonder you're tired and nervous," Francine went on. "If I was a man, I'd be tired and nervous, too. I guess God made women so men could relax and be treated like little babies from time to time." She was more than satisfied with this arrangement.

Dwayne snuffled. The air was rich with the smell of raspberries, which was the perfume in the disinfectant and roach-killer the motel used.

Francine mused about the prison, where the guards were all white and most of the prisoners were black. "Is it true," she said, "that nobody ever escaped from there?"

"It's true," said Dwayne.

• • •

"When was the last time they used the electric chair?" said Francine. She was asking about a device in the basement of the prison, which looked like this:

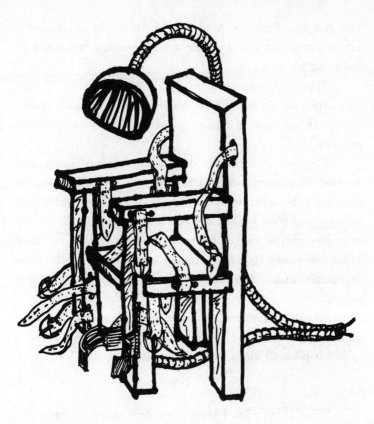

The purpose of it was to kill people by jazzing them with more electricity than their bodies could stand. Dwayne Hoover had seen it twice—once during a tour of the prison by members of the Chamber of Commerce years ago, and then again when it was actually used on a black human being he knew.

• • •

Dwayne tried to remember when the last execution took place at Shepherdstown. Executions had become unpopular. There were signs that they might become popular again.

159

Dwayne and Francine tried to remember the most recent electrocution anywhere in the country which had stuck in their minds.

They remembered the double execution of a man and wife for treason. The couple had supposedly given secrets about how to make a hydrogen bomb to another country.

They remembered the double execution of a man and woman who were lovers. The man was good-looking and sexy, and he used to seduce ugly old women who had money, and then he and the woman he really loved would kill the women for their money. The woman he really loved was young, but she certainly wasn't pretty in the conventional sense. She weighed two hundred and forty pounds.

Francine wondered out loud why a thin, good-looking young man would love a woman that heavy.

"It takes all kinds," said Dwayne.

· · ·

"You know what I keep thinking?" said Francine.

Dwayne snuffled.

"This would be a very good location for a Colonel Sanders Kentucky Fried Chicken franchise."

Dwayne's relaxed body contracted as though each muscle in it had been stung by a drop of lemon juice.

Here was the problem: Dwayne wanted Francine to love him for his body and soul, not for what his money could buy. He thought Francine was hinting that he should buy her a Colonel Sanders Kentucky Fried Chicken franchise, which was a scheme for selling fried chicken.

A chicken was a flightless bird which looked like this:

The idea was to kill it and pull out all its feathers, and cut off its head and feet and scoop out its internal organs—and then chop it into pieces and fry the pieces, and put the pieces in a waxed paper bucket with a lid on it, so it looked like this:

•   •   •

Francine, who had been so proud of her capacity to make Dwayne relax, was now ashamed to have made him tighten up again. He was as rigid as an ironing board. "Oh my God—" she said, "what's the matter now?"

"If you're going to ask me for presents," said Dwayne, "just do me a favor—and don't hint around right after we've made love. Let's keep love-making and presents separate. O.K.?"

"I don't even know what you think I asked for," said Francine.

Dwayne mimicked her cruelly in a falsetto voice: " 'I don't even know what you think I asked you for,' " he said. He looked about as pleasant and relaxed as a coiled rattlesnake now. It was his bad chemicals, of course, which were compelling him to look like that. A real rattlesnake looked like this:

The Creator of the Universe had put a rattle on its tail. The Creator had also given it front teeth which were hypodermic syringes filled with deadly poison.

• • •

Sometimes I wonder about the Creator of the Universe.

• • •

Another animal invented by the Creator of the Universe was a Mexican beetle which could make a blank-cartridge gun out of its rear end. It could detonate its own farts and knock over other bugs with shock waves.

163

Word of Honor—I read about it in an article on strange animals in *Diners' Club Magazine*.

• • •

So Francine got off the bed in order not to share it with the seeming rattlesnake. She was aghast. All she could say over and over again was, "You're my *man*. You're my *man*." This meant that she was willing to agree about anything with Dwayne, to do anything for him, no matter how difficult or disgusting, to think up nice things to do for him that he didn't even notice, to die for him, if necessary, and so on.

She honestly tried to live that way. She couldn't imagine anything better to do. So she fell apart when Dwayne persisted in his nastiness. He told her that every woman was a whore, and every whore had her price, and Francine's price was what a Colonel Sanders Kentucky Fried Chicken franchise would cost, which would be well over one hundred thousand dollars by the time adequate parking and exterior lighting and all that was taken into consideration, and so on.

Francine replied in blubbering gibberish that she had never wanted the franchise for herself, that she had wanted it for Dwayne, that everything she wanted was for Dwayne. Some of the words came through. "I thought of all the people who come out here to visit their relatives in prison, and I realized how most of them were black, and I thought how much black people liked fried chicken," she said.

"So you want me to open a Nigger joint?" said Dwayne. And so on. So Francine now had the distinction of being the second close associate of Dwayne's who discovered how vile he could be.

"Harry LeSabre was right," said Francine. She was backed up against the cement block wall of the motel room now, with her fingers spread over her mouth. Harry LeSabre, of course, was Dwayne's transvestite sales manager. "He said you'd changed," said Francine. She made a cage of fingers around her mouth. "Oh, God, Dwayne—" she said, "you've changed, you've changed."

"Maybe it was time!" said Dwayne. "I never felt better in my life!" And so on.

• • •

Harry LeSabre was at that moment crying, too. He was at home—in bed. He had a purple velvet sheet over his head. He was well-to-do. He had invested in the stock market very intelligently and luckily over the years. He had bought one hundred shares of Xerox, for instance, for eight dollars a share. With the passage of time, his shares had become one hundred times as valuable, simply lying in the total darkness and silence of a safe-deposit box.

There was a lot of money magic like that going on. It was almost as though some blue fairy were flitting about that part of the dying planet, waving her magic wand over certain deeds and bonds and stock certificates.

• • •

Harry's wife, Grace, was stretched out on a chaise longue at some distance from the bed. She was smoking a small cigar in a long holder made from the legbone of a stork. A stork was a large European bird, about half the size of a Bermuda Ern. Children who wanted to know where babies came from were sometimes told that they were brought by storks. People who told their children such a thing felt that their children were too young to think intelligently about wide-open beavers and all that.

And there were actually pictures of storks delivering babies on birth announcements and in cartoons and so on, for children to see. A typical one might look like this:

Dwayne Hoover and Harry LeSabre saw pictures like that when they were very little boys. They believed them, too.

. . .

Grace LeSabre expressed her contempt for the good opinion of Dwayne Hoover, which her husband felt he had lost. "Fuck Dwayne Hoover," she said. "Fuck Midland City. Let's sell the God damn Xerox stock and buy a condominium on Maui." Maui was one of the Hawaiian Islands. It was widely believed to be a paradise.

"Listen," said Grace, "we're the only white people in Midland City with any kind of sex life, as nearly as I can tell. You're not a freak. Dwayne Hoover's the freak! How many orgasms do you think he has a month?"

"I don't know," said Harry from his humid tent.

Dwayne's monthly orgasm rate on the average over the past ten years, which included the last years of his marriage, was two and one-quarter. Grace's guess was close. "One point five," she said. Her own monthly average over the same period was eighty-seven. Her husband's average was thirty-six. He had been slowing up in recent years, which was one of many reasons he had for feeling panicky.

Grace now spoke loudly and scornfully about Dwayne's marriage. "He was so scared of sex," she said, "he married a woman who had never heard of the subject, who was guaranteed to destroy herself, if she ever *did* hear about it." And so on. "Which she finally did," she said.

• • •

"Can the reindeer hear you?" said Harry.

"Fuck the reindeer," said Grace. Then she added, "No, the reindeer cannot hear." *Reindeer* was their code word for the black maid, who was far away in the kitchen at the time. It was their code word for black people in general. It allowed them to speak of the black problem in the city, which was a big one, without giving offense to any black person who might overhear.

"The reindeer's asleep—or reading the *Black Panther Digest*," she said.

• • •

The reindeer problem was essentially this: Nobody white had much use for black people anymore—except for the gangsters who sold the black people used cars and dope and furniture. Still, the reindeer went on reproducing. There were these useless, big black animals everywhere, and a lot of them had very bad dispositions. They were given small amounts of money every month, so they wouldn't have to steal. There was talk of giving them very cheap dope, too—to keep them listless and cheerful, and uninterested in reproduction.

The Midland City Police Department, and the Midland County Sheriff's Department, were composed mainly of white men. They had racks and racks of sub-machine guns and twelve-gauge automatic shotguns for an open season on reindeer, which was bound to come.

"Listen—I'm serious," said Grace to Harry. "This is the asshole of the Universe. Let's split to a condominium on Maui and *live* for a change."

So they did.

• • •

Dwayne's bad chemicals meanwhile changed his manner toward Francine from nastiness to pitiful dependency. He apologized to her for ever thinking that she wanted a Colonel Sanders Kentucky Fried Chicken franchise. He gave her full credit for unflagging unselfishness. He begged her to just hold him for a while, which she did.

"I'm so confused," he said.

"We all are," she said. She cradled his head against her breasts.

"I've got to talk to somebody," said Dwayne.

"You can talk to Mommy, if you want," said Francine. She meant that *she* was *Mommy*.

"Tell me what life is all about," Dwayne begged her fragrant bosom.

"Only God knows that," said Francine.

• • •

Dwayne was silent for a while. And then he told her haltingly about a trip he had made to the headquarters of the Pontiac Division of General Motors at Pontiac, Michigan, only three months after his wife ate Drāno.

"We were given a tour of all the research facilities," he said. The thing that impressed him most, he said, was a series of laboratories and out-of-doors test areas where various parts of automobiles and even entire automobiles were destroyed. Pontiac scientists set upholstery on fire, threw gravel at windshields, snapped crankshafts and drive-shafts, staged head-on collisions, tore gearshift levers out by the roots, ran engines at high speeds with almost no lubrication, opened and closed glove compartment doors a hundred times a minute for days, cooled dashboard clocks to within a few degrees of absolute zero, and so on.

"Everything you're not supposed to do to a car, they did to a car," Dwayne said to Francine. "And I'll never forget the sign on the front door of the building where all that torture went on." Here was the sign Dwayne described to Francine:

"I saw that sign," said Dwayne, "and I couldn't help wondering if that was what God put me on Earth for—to find out how much a man could take without breaking."

• • •

"I've lost my way," said Dwayne. "I need somebody to take me by the hand and lead me out of the woods."

"You're tired," she said. "Why wouldn't you be tired? You work *so* hard. I feel sorry for men, they work so hard. You want to sleep for a while?"

"I can't sleep," said Dwayne, "until I get some answers."

"You want to go to a doctor?" said Francine.

"I don't want to hear the kinds of things doctors say," said Dwayne. "I want to talk to somebody brand new. Francine," he said, and he dug his fingers into her soft arm, "I want to hear new things from new people. I've heard everything anybody in Midland City ever said, ever *will* say. It's got to be somebody new."

"Like who?" said Francine.

"I don't know," said Dwayne. "Somebody from Mars, maybe."

"We could go to some other city," said Francine.

"They're all like here. They're all the same," said Dwayne.

Francine had an idea. "What about all these painters and writers and composers coming to town?" she said. "You never talked to anybody like that before. Maybe you should talk to one of them. They don't think like other people."

"I've tried everything else," said Dwayne. He brightened. He nodded. "You're right! The Festival could give me a brand new viewpoint on life!" he said.

"That's what it's for," said Francine. "*Use* it!"

"I *will*," said Dwayne. This was a bad mistake.

• • •

Kilgore Trout, hitchhiking westward, ever westward, had meanwhile become a passenger in a Ford *Galaxie*. The man at the controls of the *Galaxie* was a traveling salesman for a device which engulfed the rear ends of trucks at loading docks. It was a telescoping tunnel of rubberized canvas, and it looked like this in action:

The idea of the gadget was to allow people in a building to load or unload trucks without losing cold air in the summertime or hot air in the wintertime to the out-of-doors.

The man in control of the *Galaxie* also sold large spools for wire and cable and rope. He also sold fire extinguishers. He was a manufacturer's representative, he explained. He was his own boss, in that he represented products whose manufacturers couldn't afford salesmen of their own.

"I make my own hours, and I pick the products I sell. The products don't sell me," he said. His name was Andy Lieber. He was thirty-two. He was white. He was a good deal overweight like so many people in the country. He was obviously a happy man. He drove like a maniac. The *Galaxie* was going ninety-two miles an hour now. "I'm one of the few remaining free men in America," he said.

He had a penis one inch in diameter and seven and a half inches long. During the past year, he had averaged twenty-two orgasms per month. This was far above the national average. His income and the value of his life insurance policies at maturity were also far above average.

• • •

Trout wrote a novel one time which he called *How You Doin'?* and it was about national averages for this and that. An advertising agency on another planet had a successful campaign for the local equivalent of Earthling peanut butter. The eye-catching part of each ad was the statement of some sort of average—the average number of children, the average size of the male sex organ on that particular planet—which was two inches long, with an inside diameter of three inches and an outside diameter of four and a quarter inches—and so on. The ads invited the readers to discover whether they were superior or inferior to the majority, in this respect or that one—whatever the respect was for that particular ad.

The ad went on to say that superior and inferior people alike ate such and such brand of peanut butter. Except that it wasn't really peanut butter on that planet. It was *Shazzbutter*.

And so on.

16

AND THE PEANUT BUTTER-EATERS on Earth were preparing to conquer the shazzbutter-eaters on the planet in the book by Kilgore Trout. By this time, the Earthlings hadn't just demolished West Virginia and Southeast Asia. They had demolished everything. So they were ready to go pioneering again.

They studied the shazzbutter-eaters by means of electronic snooping, and determined that they were too numerous and proud and resourceful ever to allow themselves to be pioneered.

So the Earthlings infiltrated the ad agency which had the shazzbutter account, and they buggered the statistics in the ads. They made the average for everything so high that everybody on the planet felt inferior to the majority in every respect.

And then the Earthling armored space ships came in and discovered the planet. Only token resistance was offered here and there, because the natives felt so below average. And then the pioneering began.

• • •

Trout asked the happy manufacturer's representative what it felt like to drive a *Galaxie,* which was the name of the car. The driver didn't hear him, and Trout let it go. It was a dumb play on words, so that Trout was asking simultaneously what it was like to drive the car and what it was like to steer something like the Milky Way, which was one hundred thousand light-years in diameter and ten thousand light-years thick. It revolved once every two hundred million years. It contained about one hundred billion stars.

And then Trout saw that a simple fire extinguisher in the *Galaxie* had this brand name:

As far as Trout knew, this word meant *higher* in a dead language. It was also a thing a fictitious mountain climber in a famous poem kept yelling as he disappeared into a blizzard up above. And it was also the trade name for wood shavings which were used to protect fragile objects inside packages.

"Why would anybody name a fire extinguisher *Excelsior*?" Trout asked the driver.

The driver shrugged. "Somebody must have liked the *sound* of it," he said.

• • •

Trout looked out at the countryside, which was smeared by high velocity. He saw this sign:

So he was getting really close to Dwayne Hoover. And, as though the Creator of the Universe or some other supernatural power were preparing him for the meeting, Trout felt the urge to thumb through his own book, *Now It Can Be Told*. This was the book which would soon turn Dwayne into a homicidal maniac.

The premise of the book was this: Life was an experiment by the Creator of the Universe, Who wanted to test a new sort of creature He was thinking of introducing into the Universe. It was a creature with the ability to make up its own mind. All the other creatures were fully-programmed robots.

The book was in the form of a long letter from The Creator of the Universe to the experimental creature. The Creator congratulated the creature and apologized for all the discomfort he had endured. The Creator invited him to a banquet in his honor in the Empire Room of the Waldorf-Astoria Hotel in New York City, where a black robot named Sammy Davis, Jr., would sing and dance.

• • •

And the experimental creature wasn't killed after the banquet. He was transferred to a virgin planet instead. Living cells were sliced from the palms of his hands, while he was unconscious. The operation didn't hurt at all.

And then the cells were stirred into a soupy sea on the virgin planet. They would evolve into ever more complicated life forms as the eons went by. Whatever shapes they assumed, they would have free will.

Trout didn't give the experimental creature a proper name. He simply called him *The Man*.

On the virgin planet, The Man was Adam and the sea was Eve.

• • •

The Man often sauntered by the sea. Sometimes he waded in his Eve. Sometimes he swam in her, but she was too soupy for an invigorating swim. She made her Adam feel sleepy and sticky afterwards, so he would dive into an icy stream that had just jumped off a mountain.

He screamed when he dived into the icy water, screamed again when he came up for air. He bloodied his shins and laughed about it when he scrambled up rocks to get out of the water.

He panted and laughed some more, and he thought of something amazing to yell. The Creator never knew what he was going to yell, since The Creator had no control over him. The Man himself got to decide what he was going to do next—and why. After a dip one day, for instance, The Man yelled this: "Cheese!"

Another time he yelled, "Wouldn't you really rather drive a Buick?"

• • •

The only other big animal on the virgin planet was an angel who visited The Man occasionally. He was a messenger and an investigator for the Creator of the Universe. He took the form of an eight hundred pound male cinnamon bear. He was a robot, too, and so was The Creator, according to Kilgore Trout.

The bear was attempting to get a line on why The Man did what he did. He would ask, for instance, "Why did you yell, 'Cheese'?"

And The Man would tell him mockingly, "Because I *felt* like it, you stupid machine."

• • •

Here is what The Man's tombstone on the virgin planet looked like at the end of the book by Kilgore Trout:

NOT EVEN
THE CREATOR
OF THE UNIVERSE
KNEW WHAT
THE MAN
WAS GOING TO SAY NEXT

PERHAPS THE MAN
WAS A BETTER UNIVERSE
IN ITS INFANCY

R.I.P.

17

Bunny Hoover, Dwayne's homosexual son, was dressing for work now. He was the piano player in the cocktail lounge of the new Holiday Inn. He was poor. He lived alone in a room without bath in the old Fairchild Hotel, which used to be fashionable. It was a flophouse now—in the most dangerous part of Midland City.

Very soon, Bunny Hoover would be seriously injured by Dwayne, would soon share an ambulance with Kilgore Trout.

• • •

Bunny was pale, the same unhealthy color of the blind fish that used to live in the bowels of Sacred Miracle Cave. Those fish were extinct. They had all turned belly-up years ago, had been flushed from the cave and into the Ohio River—to turn belly-up, to go *bang* in the noonday sun.

Bunny avoided the sunshine, too. And the water from the taps of Midland City was becoming more poisonous every day. He ate very little. He prepared his own food in his room.

The preparation was simple, since vegetables and fruits were all he ate, and he munched them raw.

He not only did without dead meat—he did without living meat, too, without friends or lovers or pets. He had once been highly popular. When he was at Prairie Military Academy, for instance, the student body was unanimous in electing him Cadet Colonel, the highest rank possible, in his senior year.

• • •

When Bunny played the piano bar at the Holiday Inn, he had many, many secrets. One of them was this: he wasn't really there. He was able to absent himself from the cocktail lounge, and from the planet itself, for that matter, by means of Transcendental Meditation. He learned this technique from Maharishi Mahesh Yogi, who once stopped off in Midland City during a world-wide lecture tour.

Maharishi Mahesh Yogi, in exchange for a new handkerchief, a piece of fruit, a bunch of flowers, and thirty-five dollars, taught Bunny to close his eyes, and to say this euphonious nonsense word to himself over and over again: "Aye-eeeeem, aye-eeeeem, aye-eeeeem." Bunny sat on the edge of his bed in the hotel room now, and he did it. "Aye-eeeeem, aye-eeeeem," he said to himself—internally. The rhythm of the chant matched one syllable with each two beats in his heart. He closed his eyes. He became a skin diver in the depths of his mind. The depths were seldom used.

His heart slowed. His respiration nearly stopped. A single word floated by in the depths. It had somehow escaped from the busier parts of his mind. It wasn't connected to anything. It floated by lazily, a translucent, scarf-like fish. The word was untroubling. Here was the word: "Blue." Here is what it looked like to Bunny Hoover:

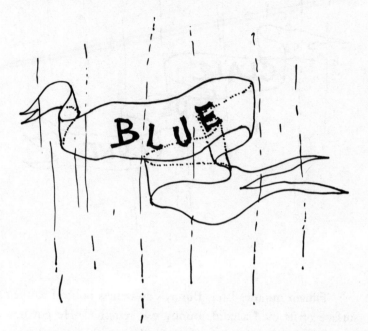

And then another lovely scarf swam by. It looked like this:

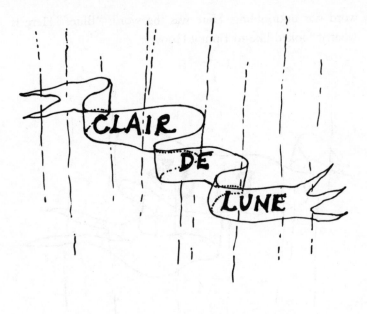

• • •

Fifteen minutes later, Bunny's awareness bobbed to the surface of its own accord. Bunny was refreshed. He got up from the bed, and he brushed his hair with the military brushes his mother had given him when he was elected Cadet Colonel so long ago.

• • •

Bunny was sent away to military school, an institution devoted to homicide and absolutely humorless obedience, when he was only ten years old. Here is why: He told Dwayne that he wished he were a woman instead of a man, because what men did was so often cruel and ugly.

• • •

Listen: Bunny Hoover went to Prairie Military Academy for eight years of uninterrupted sports, buggery and Fascism. Buggery consisted of sticking one's penis in somebody else's asshole or mouth, or having it done to one by somebody else. Fascism was a fairly popular political philosophy which made sacred whatever nation and race the philosopher happened to belong to. It called for an autocratic, centralized government, headed up by a dictator. The dictator had to be obeyed, no matter what he told somebody to do.

And Bunny would bring new medals with him every time he came home for vacation. He could fence and box and wrestle and swim, he could shoot a rifle and a pistol, fight with bayonets, ride a horse, creep and crawl through shrubbery, peek around corners without being seen.

He would show off his medals, and his mother would tell him when his father was out of hearing that she was becoming unhappier with each passing day. She would hint that Dwayne was a monster. It wasn't true. It was all in her head.

She would begin to tell Bunny what was so vile about Dwayne, but she always stopped short. "You're too young to hear about such things," she'd say, even when Bunny was sixteen years old. "There's nothing you or anybody could do about them anyway." She would pretend to lock her lips with a key, and then whisper to Bunny, "There are secrets I will carry to my grave."

Her biggest secret, of course, was one that Bunny didn't detect until she knocked herself off with Drāno. Celia Hoover was crazy as a bedbug.

My mother was, too.

• • •

Listen: Bunny's mother and my mother were different sorts of human beings, but they were both beautiful in exotic ways, and they both boiled over with chaotic talk about love and peace and wars and evil and desperation, of better days coming by and by, of worse days coming by and by. And both our mothers committed suicide. Bunny's mother ate Drāno. My mother ate sleeping pills, which wasn't nearly as horrible.

• • •

And Bunny's mother and my mother had one really bizarre symptom in common: neither one could stand to have her picture taken. They were usually fine in the daytime. They usually concealed their frenzies until late at night. But, if somebody aimed a camera at either one of them during the daytime, the mother who was aimed at would crash down on her knees and protect her head with her arms, as though somebody was about to club her to death. It was a scary and pitiful thing to see.

• • •

At least Bunny's mother taught him how to control a piano, which was a music machine. At least Bunny Hoover's mother taught him a trade. A good piano controller could get a job making music in cocktail lounges almost anywhere in the world, and Bunny was a good one. His military training was useless, despite all the medals he won. The armed forces knew he was a homosexual, that he was certain to fall in love with other fighting men, and the armed forces didn't want to put up with such love affairs.

• • •

So Bunny Hoover now got ready to practice his trade. He slipped a black velvet dinner jacket over a black turtleneck sweater now. Bunny looked out his only window at the alleyway. The better rooms afforded views of Fairchild Park, where there had been fifty-six murders in the past two years. Bunny's room was on the second floor, so his window framed a piece of the blank brick side of what used to be the Keedsler Opera House.

There was an historical marker on the front of the former opera house. Not many people could understand it, but this is what it said:

The Opera House used to be the home of the Midland City Symphony Orchestra, which was an amateur group of music enthusiasts. But they became homeless in 1927, when the Opera House became a motion picture house, *The Bannister*. The orchestra remained homeless, too, until the Mildred Barry Memorial Center for the Arts went up.

And *The Bannister* was the city's leading movie house for many years, until it was engulfed by the high crime district, which was moving north all the time. So it wasn't a theater anymore, even though there were still busts of Shakespeare and Mozart and so on gazing down from niches in the walls inside.

The stage was still in there, too, but it was crowded with dinette sets now. The Empire Furniture Company had taken over the premises now. It was gangster-controlled.

• • •

The nickname for Bunny's neighborhood was *Skid Row*. Every American town of any size had a neighborhood with the same nickname: Skid Row. It was a place where people who didn't have any friends or relatives or property or usefulness or ambition were supposed to go.

People like that would be treated with disgust in other neighborhoods, and policemen would keep them moving. They were as easy to move, usually, as toy balloons.

And they would drift hither and yon, like balloons filled with some gas slightly heavier than air, until they came to rest in Skid Row, against the foundations of the old Fairchild Hotel.

They could snooze and mumble to each other all day long. They could beg. They could get drunk. The basic scheme was this one: they were to stay there and not bother anybody anywhere else—until they were murdered for thrills, or until they were frozen to death by the wintertime.

. . .

Kilgore Trout wrote a story one time about a town which decided to tell derelicts where they were and what was about to happen to them by putting up actual street signs like this:

Bunny now smiled at himself in the mirror, in the *leak.*

He called himself to attention for a moment, became again the insufferably brainless, humorless, heartless soldier he had learned to be in military school. He murmured the motto of the school, a motto he used to have to shout about a hundred times a day—at dawn, at meals, at the start of every class, at games, at bayonet practice, at sunset, at bedtime:

"Can do," he said. "Can do."

18

THE *GALAXIE* in which Kilgore Trout was a passenger was on the Interstate now, close to Midland City. It was creeping. It was trapped in rush hour traffic from Barrytron and Western Electric and Prairie Mutual. Trout looked up from his reading, saw a billboard which said this:

So Sacred Miracle Cave had become a part of the past.

• • •

As an old, old man, Trout would be asked by Dr. Thor Lembrig, the Secretary-General of the United Nations, if he feared the future. He would give this reply:

"Mr. Secretary-General, it is the *past* which scares the bejesus out of me."

• • •

Dwayne Hoover was only four miles away. He was sitting alone on a zebra-skin banquette in the cocktail lounge of the new Holiday Inn. It was dark in there, and quiet, too. The glare and uproar of rush hour traffic on the Interstate was blocked out by thick drapes of crimson velvet. On each table was a hurricane lamp with a candle inside, although the air was still.

On each table was a bowl of dry-roasted peanuts, too, and a sign which allowed the staff to refuse service to anyone who was inharmonious with the mood of the lounge. Here is what it said:

• • •

Bunny Hoover was controlling the piano. He had not looked up when his father came in. Neither had his father glanced in his direction. They had not exchanged greetings for many years.

Bunny went on playing his white man's blues. They were slow and tinkling, with capricious silences here and there. Bunny's blues had some of the qualities of a music box, a tired music box. They tinkled, stopped, then reluctantly, torpidly, they managed a few tinkles more.

Bunny's mother used to collect tinkling music boxes, among other things.

• • •

Listen: Francine Pefko was at Dwayne's automobile agency next door. She was catching up on all the work she should have done that afternoon. Dwayne would beat her up very soon.

And the only other person on the property with her as she typed and filed was Wayne Hoobler, the black parolee, who still lurked among the used cars. Dwayne would try to beat him up, too, but Wayne was a genius at dodging blows.

Francine was pure machinery at the moment, a machine made of meat—a typing machine, a filing machine.

Wayne Hoobler, on the other hand, had nothing machine-like to do. He ached to be a useful machine. The used cars were all locked up tight for the night. Now and then aluminum propellors on a wire overhead would be turned by a lazy breeze, and Wayne would respond to them as best he could. "Go," he would say to them. "Spin 'roun'."

• • •

He established a sort of relationship with the traffic on the Interstate, too, appreciating its changing moods. "Everybody goin' home," he said during the rush hour jam. "Everybody home now," he said later on, when the traffic thinned out. Now the sun was going down.

"Sun goin' down," said Wayne Hoobler. He had no clues as to where to go next. He supposed without minding much that he might die of exposure that night. He had never seen death by exposure, had never been threatened by it, since he had so seldom been out-of-doors. He knew of death by exposure because the papery voice of the little radio in his cell told of people's dying of exposure from time to time.

He missed that papery voice. He missed the clash of steel doors. He missed the bread and the stew and the pitchers of milk and coffee. He missed fucking other men in the mouth and the asshole, and being fucked in the mouth and the asshole, and jerking off—and fucking cows in the prison dairy, all events in a normal sex life on the planet, as far as he knew.

Here would be a good tombstone for Wayne Hoobler when he died:

BLACK
JAILBIRD
HE ADAPTED
TO WHAT THERE
WAS TO ADAPT
TO.

• • •

The dairy at the prison provided milk and cream and butter and cheese and ice cream not only for the prison and the County Hospital. It sold its products to the outside world, too. Its trademark didn't mention prison. This was it:

Wayne couldn't read very well. The words *Hawaii* and *Hawaiian,* for instance, appeared in combination with more familiar words and symbols in signs painted on the windows of the showroom and on the windshields of some used cars. Wayne tried to decode the mysterious words phonetically, without any satisfaction. "Wahee-io," he would say, and "Hoo-he-woo-hi," and so on.

• • •

Wayne Hoobler smiled now, not because he was happy but because, with so little to do, he thought he might as well show off his teeth. They were excellent teeth. The Adult Correctional Institution at Shepherdstown was proud of its dentistry program.

It was such a famous dental program, in fact, that it had been written up in medical journals and in the *Reader's Digest,* which was the dying planet's most popular magazine. The theory behind the program was that many ex-convicts could not or would not get jobs because of their appearances, and good looks began with good teeth.

The program was so famous, in fact, that police even in neighboring states, when they picked up a poor man with expensively maintained teeth, fillings and bridgework and all that, were likely to ask him, "All right, boy—how many years you spend in Shepherdstown?"

• • •

Wayne Hoobler heard some of the orders which a waitress called to the bartender in the cocktail lounge. Wayne heard her call, "Gilbey's and quinine, with a twist." He had no idea what that was—or a Manhattan or a brandy Alexander or a sloe gin fizz. "Give me a Johnnie Walker Rob Roy," she called, "and a Southern Comfort on the rocks, and a Bloody Mary with Wolfschmidt's."

Wayne's only experiences with alcohol had had to do with drinking cleaning fluids and eating shoe polish and so on. He had no fondness for alcohol.

• • •

"Give me a Black and White and water," he heard the waitress say, and Wayne should have pricked up his ears at that. That particular drink wasn't for any ordinary person. That drink was for the person who had created all Wayne's misery to date, who could kill him or make him a millionaire or send him back to prison or do whatever he damn pleased with Wayne. That drink was for me.

• • •

I had come to the Arts Festival incognito. I was there to watch a confrontation between two human beings I had created: Dwayne Hoover and Kilgore Trout. I was not eager to be recognized. The waitress lit the hurricane lamp on my table. I pinched out the flame with my fingers. I had bought a pair of sunglasses at a Holiday Inn outside of Ashtabula, Ohio, where I spent the night before. I wore them in the darkness now. They looked like this:

The lenses were silvered, were mirrors to anyone looking my way. Anyone wanting to know what my eyes were like was confronted with his or her own twin reflections. Where other people in the cocktail lounge had eyes, I had two holes into another universe. I had *leaks*.

• • •

There was a book of matches on my table, next to my Pall Mall cigarettes.

Here is the message on the book of matches, which I read an hour and a half later, while Dwayne was beating the daylights out of Francine Pefko:

"It's easy to make $100 a week in your spare time by showing comfortable, latest style Mason shoes to your friends. EVERYBODY goes for Mason shoes with their many special comfort features! We'll send FREE moneymaking kit so you can run your business from home. We'll even tell you how you can earn shoes FREE OF COST as a bonus for taking profitable orders!"

And so on.

. . .

"This is a very bad book you're writing," I said to myself behind my *leaks*.

"I know," I said.

"You're afraid you'll kill yourself the way your mother did," I said.

"I know," I said.

. . .

There in the cocktail lounge, peering out through my leaks at a world of my own invention, I mouthed this word: *schizophrenia*.

The sound and appearance of the word had fascinated me for many years. It sounded and looked to me like a human being sneezing in a blizzard of soapflakes.

I did not and do not know for certain that I have that disease. This much I knew and know: I was making myself hideously uncomfortable by not narrowing my attention to details of life which were immediately important, and by refusing to believe what my neighbors believed.

• • •

I am better now.

Word of honor: I am better now.

• • •

I was really sick for a while, though. I sat there in a cocktail lounge of my own invention, and I stared through my *leaks* at a white cocktail waitress of my own invention. I named her Bonnie MacMahon. I had her bring Dwayne Hoover his customary drink, which was a House of Lords martini with a twist of lemon peel. She was a longtime acquaintance of Dwayne's. Her husband was a guard in the Sexual Offenders' Wing of the Adult Correctional Institution. Bonnie had to work as a waitress because her husband lost all their money by investing it in a car wash in Shepherdstown.

Dwayne had advised them not to do it. Here is how Dwayne knew her and her husband Ralph: They had bought nine Pontiacs from him over the past sixteen years.

"We're a Pontiac family," they'd say.

Bonnie made a joke now as she served him his martini. She made the same joke every time she served anybody a martini. "Breakfast of Champions," she said.

• • •

The expression "Breakfast of Champions" is a registered trademark of General Mills, Inc., for use on a breakfast cereal product. The use of the identical expression as the title for this book as well as throughout the book is not intended to indicate an association with or sponsorship by General Mills, nor is it intended to disparage their fine products.

. . .

Dwayne was hoping that some of the distinguished visitors to the Arts Festival, who were all staying at the Inn, would come into the cocktail lounge. He wanted to talk to them, if he could, to discover whether they had truths about life which he had never heard before. Here is what he hoped new truths might do for him: enable him to laugh at his troubles, to go on living, and to keep out of the North Wing of the Midland County General Hospital, which was for lunatics.

While he waited for an artist to appear, he consoled himself with the only artistic creation of any depth and mystery which was stored in his head. It was a poem he had been forced to learn by heart during his sophomore year in Sugar Creek High School, the elite white high school at the time. Sugar Creek High was a Nigger high school now. Here was the poem:

> *The Moving Finger writes; and, having writ,*
> *Moves on: nor all your Piety nor Wit*
> *Shall lure it back to cancel half a Line*
> *Nor all your Tears wash out a Word of it.*

Some poem!

. . .

And Dwayne was so open to new suggestions about the meaning of life that he was easily hypnotized. So, when he looked down into his martini, he was put into a trance by dancing myriads of winking eyes on the surface of his drink. The eyes were beads of lemon oil.

Dwayne missed it when two distinguished visitors to the Arts Festival came in and sat down on barstools next to Bunny's piano. They were white. They were Beatrice Keedsler, the Gothic novelist, and Rabo Karabekian, the minimal painter.

Bunny's piano, a Steinway baby grand, was armored with pumpkin-colored Formica and ringed with stools. People could eat and drink from the piano. On the previous Thanksgiving, a family of eleven had had Thanksgiving dinner served on the piano. Bunny played.

• • •

"This *has* to be the asshole of the Universe," said Rabo Karabekian, the minimal painter.

Beatrice Keedsler, the Gothic novelist, had grown up in Midland City. "I was petrified about coming home after all these years," she said to Karabekian.

"Americans are always afraid of coming home," said Karabekian, "with good reason, may I say."

"They *used* to have good reason," said Beatrice, "but not anymore. The past has been rendered harmless. I would tell any wandering American now, 'Of course you can go home again, and as often as you please. It's just a motel.' "

• • •

Traffic on the westbound barrel of the Interstate had come to a halt a mile east of the new Holiday Inn—because of a fatal accident on Exit 10A. Drivers and passengers got out of their cars—to stretch their legs and find out, if they could, what the trouble was up ahead.

Kilgore Trout was among those who got out. He learned from others that the new Holiday Inn was within easy walking distance. So he gathered up his parcels from the front seat of the *Galaxie*. He thanked the driver, whose name he had forgotten, and he began to trudge.

He also began to assemble in his mind a system of beliefs which would be appropriate to his narrow mission in Midland City, which was to show provincials, who were bent on exalting creativity, a would-be creator who had failed and failed. He paused in his trudge to examine himself in the rearview mirror, the rearview *leak,* of a truck locked up in traffic. The tractor was pulling two trailers instead of one. Here was the message the owners of the rig saw fit to shriek at human beings wherever it went:

Trout's image in the *leak* was as shocking as he had hoped it would be. He had not washed up after his drubbing by *The Pluto Gang,* so there was caked blood on one earlobe, and more under his left nostril. There was dog shit on a shoulder of his coat. He had collapsed into dog shit on the handball court under the Queensboro Bridge after the robbery.

By an unbelievable coincidence, that shit came from the wretched greyhound belonging to a girl I knew.

• • •

The girl with the greyhound was an assistant lighting director for a musical comedy about American history, and she kept her poor greyhound, who was named *Lancer,* in a one-room apartment fourteen feet wide and twenty-six feet long, and six flights of stairs above street level. His entire life was devoted to unloading his excrement at the proper time and place. There were two proper places to put it: in the gutter outside the door seventy-two steps below, with the traffic whizzing by, or in a roasting pan his mistress kept in front of the Westinghouse refrigerator.

Lancer had a very small brain, but he must have suspected from time to time, just as Wayne Hoobler did, that some kind of terrible mistake had been made.

●　●　●

Trout trudged onward, a stranger in a strange land. His pilgrimage was rewarded with new wisdom, which would never have been his had he remained in his basement in Cohoes. He learned the answer to a question many human beings were asking themselves so frantically: "What's blocking traffic on the westbound barrel of the Midland City stretch of the Interstate?"

The scales fell from the eyes of Kilgore Trout. He saw the explanation: a *Queen of the Prairies* milk truck was lying on its side, blocking the flow. It had been hit hard by a ferocious 1971 Chevrolet *Caprice* two-door. The Chevy had jumped the median divider strip. The Chevy's passenger hadn't used his seat belt. He had shot right through the shatterproof windshield. He was lying dead now in the concrete trough containing Sugar Creek. The Chevy's driver was also dead. He had been skewered by the post of his steering wheel.

The Chevy's passenger was bleeding blood as he lay dead in Sugar Creek. The milk truck was bleeding milk. Milk and blood were about to be added to the composition of the stinking ping-pong balls which were being manufactured in the bowels of Sacred Miracle Cave.

19

I **WAS ON A PAR** with the Creator of the Universe there in the dark in the cocktail lounge. I shrunk the Universe to a ball exactly one light-year in diameter. I had it explode. I had it disperse itself again.

Ask me a question, any question. How old is the Universe? It is one half-second old, but that half-second has lasted one quintillion years so far. Who created it? Nobody created it. It has always been here.

What is time? It is a serpent which eats its tail, like this:

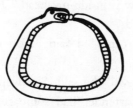

This is the snake which uncoiled itself long enough to offer Eve the apple, which looked like this:

What was the apple which Eve and Adam ate? It was the Creator of the Universe.

And so on.

Symbols can be so beautiful, sometimes.

. . .

Listen:

The waitress brought me another drink. She wanted to light my hurricane lamp again. I wouldn't let her. "Can you see anything in the dark, with your sunglasses on?" she asked me.

"The big show is inside my head," I said.

"Oh," she said.

"I can tell fortunes," I said. "You want your fortune told?"

"Not right now," she said. She went back to the bar, and she and the bartender had some sort of conversation about me, I think. The bartender took several anxious looks in my direction. All he could see were the *leaks* over my eyes. I did not worry about his asking me to leave the establishment.

I had created him, after all. I gave him a name: Harold Newcomb Wilbur. I awarded him the Silver Star, the Bronze Star, the Soldier's Medal, the Good Conduct Medal, and a Purple Heart with two Oak-Leaf Clusters, which made him the second most decorated veteran in Midland City. I put all his medals under his handkerchiefs in a dresser drawer.

He won all those medals in the Second World War, which was staged by robots so that Dwayne Hoover could give a free-willed reaction to such a holocaust. The war was such an extravaganza that there was scarcely a robot anywhere who didn't have a part to play. Harold Newcomb Wilbur got his medals for killing Japanese, who were yellow robots. They were fueled by rice.

And he went on staring at me, even though I wanted to stop him now. Here was the thing about my control over the characters I created: I could only guide their movements approximately, since they were such big animals. There was inertia to overcome. It wasn't as though I was connected to them by steel wires. It was more as though I was connected to them by stale rubberbands.

So I made the green telephone in back of the bar ring. Harold Newcomb Wilbur answered it, but he kept his eyes on me. I had to think fast about who was on the other end of the telephone. I put the first most decorated veteran in Midland City on the other end. He had a penis eight hundred miles long and two hundred and ten miles in diameter, but practically all of it was in the fourth dimension. He got his medals in the war in Viet Nam. He had also fought yellow robots who ran on rice.

"Cocktail lounge," said Harold Newcomb Wilbur.

"Hal—?"

"Yes?"

"This is Ned Lingamon."

"I'm busy."

"Don't hang up. The cops got me down at City Jail. They only let me have one call, so I called you."

"Why me?"

"You're the only friend I got left."

"What they got you in for?"

"They say I killed my baby."

And so on.

This man, who was white, had all the medals Harold Newcomb Wilbur had, plus the highest decoration for heroism which an American soldier could receive, which looked like this:

He had now also committed the lowest crime which an American could commit, which was to kill his own child. Her name was Cynthia Anne, and she certainly didn't live very long before she was made dead again. She got killed for crying and crying. She wouldn't shut up.

First she drove her seventeen-year-old mother away with all her demands, and then her father killed her.

And so on.

• • •

As for the fortune I might have told for the waitress, this was it: "You will be swindled by termite exterminators and not even know it. You will buy steel-belted radial tires for the front wheels of your car. Your cat will be killed by a motorcyclist named Headley Thomas, and you will get another cat. Arthur, your brother in Atlanta, will find eleven dollars in a taxicab."

• • •

I might have told Bunny Hoover's fortune, too: "Your father will become extremely ill, and you will respond so grotesquely that there will be talk of putting you in the booby hatch, too. You will stage scenes in the hospital waiting room, telling doctors and nurses that you are to blame for your father's disease. You will blame yourself for trying for so many years to kill him with hatred. You will redirect your hatred. You will hate your mom."

And so on.

And I had Wayne Hoobler, the black ex-convict, stand bleakly among the garbage cans outside the back door of the Inn, and examine the currency which had been given to him at the prison gate that morning. He had nothing else to do.

He studied the pyramid with the blazing eye on top. He

wished he had more information about the pyramid and the eye. There was so much to learn!

Wayne didn't even know the Earth revolved around the Sun. He thought the Sun revolved around the Earth, because it certainly looked that way.

A truck sizzled by on the Interstate, seemed to cry out in pain to Wayne, because he read the message on the side of it phonetically. The message told Wayne that the truck was in agony, as it hauled things from here to there. This was the message, and Wayne said it out loud:

. . .

Here was what was going to happen to Wayne in about four days—because I wanted it to happen to him: He would be picked up and questioned by policemen, because he was behaving suspiciously outside the back gate of Barrytron, Ltd., which was involved in super-secret weapons work. They thought at first that he might be pretending to be stupid and ignorant, that he might, in fact, be a cunning spy for the Communists.

A check of his fingerprints and his wonderful dental work proved that he was who he said he was. But there was still something else he had to explain: What was he doing with a membership card in the Playboy Club of America, made out in the name of Paulo di Capistrano? He had found it in a garbage can in back of the new Holiday Inn.

And so on.

. . .

And it was time now for me to have Rabo Karabekian, the minimalist painter, and Beatrice Keedsler, the novelist, say and do some more stuff for the sake of this book. I did not want to spook them by staring at them as I worked their controls, so I pretended to be absorbed in drawing pictures on my tabletop with a damp fingertip.

I drew the Earthling symbol for *nothingness,* which was this:

I drew the Earthling symbol for *everything,* which was this:

Dwayne Hoover and Wayne Hoobler knew the first one, but not the second one. And now I drew a symbol in vanishing mist which was bitterly familiar to Dwayne but not to Wayne. This was it:

DRĀNO

And now I drew a symbol whose meaning Dwayne had known for a few years in school, a meaning which had since eluded him. The symbol would have looked like the end of a table in a prison dining hall to Wayne. It represented the ratio of the circumference of a circle to its diameter. This ratio could also be expressed as a number, and even as Dwayne and Wayne and Karabekian and Beatrice Keedsler and all the rest of us went about our business, Earthling scientists were monotonously radioing that number into outer space. The idea was to show other inhabited planets, in case they were listening, how intelligent we were. We had tortured circles until they coughed up this symbol of their secret lives:

$$\pi$$

. . .

And I made an invisible duplicate on my Formica tabletop of a painting by Rabo Karabekian, entitled *The Temptation of Saint Anthony*. My duplicate was a miniature of the real thing, and mine was not in color, but I had captured the picture's form and the spirit, too. This is what I drew.

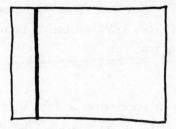

The original was twenty feet wide and sixteen feet high. The field was *Hawaiian Avocado,* a green wall paint manufactured by the O'Hare Paint and Varnish Company in Hellertown, Pennsylvania. The vertical stripe was dayglo orange reflecting tape. This was the most expensive piece of art, not counting buildings and tombstones, and not counting the statue of Abraham Lincoln in front of the old Nigger high school.

It was a scandal what the painting cost. It was the first purchase for the permanent collection of the Mildred Barry Memorial Center for the Arts. Fred T. Barry, the Chairman of the Board of Barrytron, Ltd., had coughed up fifty thousand dollars of his own for the picture.

Midland City was outraged. So was I.

• • •

So was Beatrice Keedsler, but she kept her dismay to herself as she sat at the piano bar with Karabekian. Karabekian, who wore a sweatshirt imprinted with the likeness of Beethoven, knew he was surrounded by people who hated him for getting so much money for so little work. He was amused.

Like everybody else in the cocktail lounge, he was softening his brain with alcohol. This was a substance produced by a tiny creature called yeast. Yeast organisms ate sugar and excreted alcohol. They killed themselves by destroying their own environment with yeast shit.

• • •

Kilgore Trout once wrote a short story which was a dialogue between two pieces of yeast. They were discussing the possible purposes of life as they ate sugar and suffocated in their own excrement. Because of their limited intelligence, they never came close to guessing that they were making champagne.

• • •

So I had Beatrice Keedsler say to Rabo Karabekian there at the piano bar, "This is a dreadful confession, but I don't even know who Saint Anthony was. Who was he, and why should anybody have wanted to tempt him?"

"I don't know, and I would hate to find out," said Karabekian.

"You have no use for truth?" said Beatrice.

"You know what truth is?" said Karabekian. "It's some crazy thing my neighbor believes. If I want to make friends with him, I ask him what he believes. He tells me, and I say, 'Yeah, yeah—ain't it the truth?'"

• • •

I had no respect whatsoever for the creative works of either the painter or the novelist. I thought Karabekian with his meaningless pictures had entered into a conspiracy with millionaires to make poor people feel stupid. I thought Beatrice Keedsler had joined hands with other old-fashioned storytellers to make people believe that life had leading characters, minor characters, significant details, insignificant details, that it had lessons to be learned, tests to be passed, and a beginning, a middle, and an end.

As I approached my fiftieth birthday, I had become more and more enraged and mystified by the idiot decisions made by my countrymen. And then I had come suddenly to pity them, for I understood how innocent and natural it was for them to behave so abominably, and with such abominable results: They were doing their best to live like people invented in story books. This was the reason Americans shot each other so often: It was a convenient literary device for ending short stories and books.

Why were so many Americans treated by their government as though their lives were as disposable as paper facial tissues? Because that was the way authors customarily treated bit-part players in their made-up tales.

And so on.

Once I understood what was making America such a dangerous, unhappy nation of people who had nothing to do with real life, I resolved to shun storytelling. I would write about life. Every person would be exactly as important as any other. All facts would also be given equal weightiness. Nothing would be left out. Let others bring order to chaos. I would bring chaos to order, instead, which I think I have done.

If all writers would do that, then perhaps citizens not in the literary trades will understand that there is no order in the world around us, that we must adapt ourselves to the requirements of chaos instead.

It is hard to adapt to chaos, but it can be done. I am living proof of that: It can be done.

• • •

Adapting to chaos there in the cocktail lounge, I now had Bonnie MacMahon, who was exactly as important as anybody else in the Universe, bring more yeast excrement to Beatrice Keedsler and Karabekian. Karabekian's drink was a Beefeater's dry martini with a twist of lemon peel, so Bonnie said to him, "Breakfast of Champions."

"That's what you said when you brought me my first martini," said Karabekian.

"I say it every time I give anybody a martini," said Bonnie.

"Doesn't that get tiresome?" said Karabekian. "Or maybe that's why people found cities in Godforsaken places like this—so they can make the same jokes over and over again, until the Bright Angel of Death stops their mouths with ashes."

"I just try to cheer people up," said Bonnie. "If that's a crime, I never heard about it till now. I'll stop saying it from now on. I beg your pardon. I did not mean to give offense."

Bonnie detested Karabekian, but she was as sweet as pie to him. She had a policy of never showing her anger about anything there in the cocktail lounge. The largest part of her income by far came from tips, and the way to get big tips was to smile, smile, smile, no matter what. Bonnie had only two goals in life now. She meant to recoup all the money her husband had lost in the car wash in Shepherdstown, and she ached to have steel-belted radial tires for the front wheels of her automobile.

Her husband, meanwhile, was at home watching professional golfers on television, and getting smashed on yeast excrement.

• • •

Saint Anthony, incidentally, was an Egyptian who founded the very first monastery, which was a place where men could live simple lives and pray often to the Creator of the Universe, without the distractions of ambition and sex and yeast excrement. Saint Anthony himself sold everything he had when he was young, and he went out into the wilderness and lived alone for twenty years.

He was often tempted during all those years of perfect solitude by visions of good times he might have had with food and men and women and children and the marketplace and so on.

His biographer was another Egyptian, Saint Athanasius, whose theories on the Trinity, the Incarnation, and the divinity of the Holy Spirit, set down three hundred years after the murder of Christ, were considered valid by Catholics even in Dwayne Hoover's time.

The Catholic high school in Midland City, in fact, was named in honor of Saint Athanasius. It was named in honor of Saint Christopher at first, but then the Pope, who was head of Catholic churches everywhere, announced that there probably never had been a Saint Christopher, so people shouldn't honor him anymore.

• • •

A black male dishwasher stepped out of the kitchen of the Inn now for a Pall Mall cigarette and some fresh air. He wore a large button on his sweat-soaked white T-shirt which said this:

There were bowls of such buttons around the Inn, for anybody to help himself to, and the dishwasher had taken one in a spirit of levity. He had no use for works of art, except for cheap and simple ones which weren't meant to live very long. His name was Eldon Robbins, and he had a penis nine inches long and two inches in diameter.

Eldon Robbins, too, had spent time in the Adult Correctional Institution, so it was easy for him to recognize Wayne Hoobler, out among the garbage cans, as a new parolee. "Welcome to the real world, Brother," he said gently and with wry lovingness to Wayne. "When was the last time you ate? This mornin'?"

Wayne shyly acknowledged that this was true. So Eldon took him through a kitchen to a long table where the kitchen staff ate. There was a television set back there, and it was on, and it showed Wayne the beheading of Queen Mary of Scotland. Everybody was all dressed up, and Queen Mary put her head on the block of her own accord.

Eldon arranged for Wayne to get a free steak and mashed potatoes and gravy and anything else he wanted, all prepared by other black men in the kitchen. There was a bowl of Arts Festival buttons on the table, and Eldon made Wayne put one on before he ate. "Wear this at all times," he told Wayne gravely, "and no harm can come to you."

• • •

Eldon revealed to Wayne a peephole, which kitchen workers had drilled through the wall and into the cocktail lounge. "When you get tarred of watchin' television," he said, "you can watch the animals in the zoo."

Eldon himself had a look through the peephole, told Wayne that there was a man seated at the piano bar who had been paid fifty thousand dollars for sticking a piece of yellow tape to a green piece of canvas. He insisted that Wayne take a *good* look at Karabekian. Wayne obeyed.

And Wayne wanted to remove his eye from the peephole after a few seconds, because he didn't have nearly enough background information for any sort of understanding of what was going on in the cocktail lounge. The candles puzzled him, for instance. He supposed that the electricity in there had failed, and that somebody had gone to change a fuse. Also, he did not know what to make of Bonnie MacMahon's costume, which consisted of white cowboy boots and black net stockings with crimson garters plainly showing across several inches of bare thigh, and a tight sequin sort of bathing suit with a puff of pink cotton pinned to its rear.

Bonnie's back was to Wayne, so he could not see that

she wore octagonal, rimless trifocals, and was a horse-faced woman forty-two years old. He could not see, either, that she was smiling, smiling, smiling, no matter how insulting Karabekian became. He could read Karabekian's lips, however. He was good at reading lips, as was anyone who had spent any time in Shepherdstown. The rule of silence was enforced in the corridors and at meals in Shepherdstown.

• • •

Karabekian was saying this to Bonnie, indicating Beatrice Keedsler with a wave of his hand: "This distinguished lady is a famous storyteller, and also a native of this railroad junction. Perhaps you could tell her some recent true stories about her birthplace."

"I don't know any," said Bonnie.

"Oh come now," said Karabekian. "Every human being in this room must be worth a great novel." He pointed at Dwayne Hoover. "What is the life story of that man?"

Bonnie limited herself to telling about Dwayne's dog, Sparky, who couldn't wag his tail. "So he has to fight all the time," she said.

"Wonderful," said Karabekian. He turned to Beatrice. "I'm sure you can use that somewhere."

"As a matter of fact, I can," said Beatrice. "That's an enchanting detail."

"The more details the better," said Karabekian. "Thank God for novelists. Thank God there are people willing to write everything down. Otherwise, so much would be forgotten!" He begged Bonnie for more true stories.

Bonnie was deceived by his enthusiasm and energized by the idea that Beatrice Keedsler honestly needed true stories for her books. "Well—" she said, "would you consider Shepherdstown part of Midland City, more or less?"

"Of course," said Karabekian, who had never heard of Shepherdstown. "What would Midland City be without Shepherdstown? And what would Shepherdstown be without Midland City?"

"Well—" said Bonnie, and she thought she had what was maybe a really good story to tell, "my husband is a guard at the Shepherdstown Adult Correctional Institution, and he used to have to keep people who were going to be electrocuted company—back when they used to electrocute people all the time. He'd play cards with them, or read parts of the Bible out loud to them, or whatever they wanted to do, and he had to keep a white man named Leroy Joyce company."

Bonnie's costume gave off a faint, fishy, queer glow as she spoke. This was because her garments were heavily impregnated with fluorescent chemicals. So was the bartender's jacket. So were the African masks on the walls. The chemicals would shine like electric signs when ultraviolet lights in the ceiling were energized. The lights weren't on just now. The bartender turned them on at random times, at his own whim, in order to give the customers a delightful and mystifying surprise.

The power for the lights and for everything electrical in Midland City, incidentally, was generated by coal from strip mines in West Virginia, through which Kilgore Trout had passed not many hours before.

• • •

"Leroy Joyce was so dumb," Bonnie went on, "he couldn't play cards. He couldn't understand the Bible. He could hardly talk. He ate his last supper, and then he sat still. He was going to be electrocuted for rape. So my husband sat out in the corridor outside the cell, and he read to himself. He heard Leroy moving around in his cell, but he didn't worry about it. And then Leroy rattled his tin cup on the bars. My husband thought Leroy wanted some more coffee. So he got up and went over and took the cup. Leroy was smiling as though everything was all right now. He wouldn't have to go to the electric chair after all. He'd cut off his whatchamacallit and put it in the cup."

• • •

This book is made up, of course, but the story I had Bonnie tell actually happened in real life—in the death house of a penitentiary in Arkansas.

As for Dwayne Hoover's dog Sparky, who couldn't wag his tail: Sparky is modeled after a dog my brother owns who has to fight all the time, because he can't wag his tail. There really is such a dog.

• • •

Rabo Karabekian asked Bonnie MacMahon to tell him something about the teen-age girl on the cover of the program for the Festival of the Arts. This was the only internationally famous human being in Midland City. She was Mary Alice Miller, the Women's Two Hundred Meter Breast Stroke Champion of the World. She was only fifteen, said Bonnie.

Mary Alice was also the Queen of the Festival of the Arts. The cover of the program showed her in a white bathing suit, with her Olympic Gold Medal hanging around her neck. The medal looked like this:

Mary Alice was smiling at a picture of Saint Sebastian, by the Spanish painter El Greco. It had been loaned to the Festival by Eliot Rosewater, the patron of Kilgore Trout. Saint Sebastian was a Roman soldier who had lived seventeen hundred years before me and Mary Alice Miller and Wayne and Dwayne and all the rest of us. He had secretly become a Christian when Christianity was against the law.

And somebody squealed on him. The Emperor Diocletian had him shot by archers. The picture Mary Alice smiled at with such uncritical bliss showed a human being who was so full of arrows that he looked like a porcupine.

Something almost nobody knew about Saint Sebastian, incidentally, since painters liked to put so many arrows into him, was that he survived the incident. He actually got well.

He walked around Rome praising Christianity and bad-mouthing the Emperor, so he was sentenced to death a second time. He was beaten to death by rods.

And so on.

And Bonnie MacMahon told Beatrice and Karabekian that Mary Alice's father, who was a member of the Parole Board out at Shepherdstown, had taught Mary Alice to swim

223

when she was eight months old, and that he had made her swim at least four hours a day, every day, since she was three.

Rabo Karabekian thought this over, and then he said loudly, so a lot of people could hear him, "What kind of a man would turn his daughter into an outboard motor?"

. . .

And now comes the spiritual climax of this book, for it is at this point that I, the author, am suddenly transformed by what I have done so far. This is why I had gone to Midland City: to be born again. And Chaos announced that it was about to give birth to a new me by putting these words in the mouth of Rabo Karabekian: "What kind of a man would turn his daughter into an outboard motor?"

Such a small remark was able to have such thundering consequences because the spiritual matrix of the cocktail lounge was in what I choose to call a *pre-earthquake condition*. Terrific forces were at work on our souls, but they could do no work, because they balanced one another so nicely.

But then a grain of sand crumbled. One force had a sudden advantage over another, and spiritual continents began to shrug and heave.

One force, surely, was the lust for money which infested so many people in the cocktail lounge. They knew what Rabo Karabekian had been paid for his painting, and they wanted fifty thousand dollars, too. They could have a lot of fun with fifty thousand dollars, or so they believed. But they had to earn money the hard way, just a few dollars at a time, instead. It wasn't right.

Another force was the fear in these same people that their lives might be ridiculous, that their entire city might be ridiculous. Now the worst had happened: Mary Alice Miller, the one thing about their city which they had supposed was ridicule-proof had just been lazily ridiculed by a man from out-of-town.

And my own pre-earthquake condition must be taken into consideration, too, since I was the one who was being reborn. Nobody else in the cocktail lounge was reborn, as far as I know. The rest got their minds changed, some of them, about the value of modern art.

As for myself: I had come to the conclusion that there was nothing sacred about myself or about any human being, that we were all machines, doomed to collide and collide and collide. For want of anything better to do, we became fans of collisions. Sometimes I wrote well about collisions, which meant I was a writing machine in good repair. Sometimes I wrote badly, which meant I was a writing machine in bad repair. I no more harbored sacredness than did a Pontiac, a mousetrap, or a South Bend Lathe.

I did not expect Rabo Karabekian to rescue me. I had created him, and he was in my opinion a vain and weak and trashy man, no artist at all. But it is Rabo Karabekian who made me the serene Earthling which I am this day.

Listen:

"What kind of a man would turn his daughter into an outboard motor?" he said to Bonnie MacMahon.

Bonnie MacMahon blew up. This was the first time she had blown up since she had come to work in the cocktail lounge. Her voice became as unpleasant as the noise of a bandsaw's cutting galvanized tin. It was *loud,* too. "Oh yeah?" she said. "Oh yeah?"

Everybody froze. Bunny Hoover stopped playing the piano. Nobody wanted to miss a word.

"You don't think much of Mary Alice Miller?" she said.

"Well, we don't think much of your painting. I've seen better pictures done by a five-year-old."

Karabekian slid off his barstool so he could face all those enemies standing up. He certainly surprised me. I expected him to retreat in a hail of olives, maraschino cherries and lemon rinds. But he was majestic up there "Listen—" he said so calmly, "I have read the editorial against my painting in your wonderful newspaper. I have read every word of the hate mail you have been thoughtful enough to send to New York."

This embarrassed people some.

"The painting did not exist until I made it," Karabekian went on. "Now that it does exist, nothing would make me happier than to have it reproduced again and again, and vastly improved upon, by all the five-year-olds in town. I would love for your children to find pleasantly and playfully what it took me many angry years to find.

"I now give you my word of honor," he went on, "that the picture your city owns shows everything about life which truly matters, with nothing left out. It is a picture of the awareness of every animal. It is the immaterial core of every animal—the 'I am' to which all messages are sent. It is all that is alive in any of us—in a mouse, in a deer, in a cocktail waitress. It is unwavering and pure, no matter what preposterous adventure may befall us. A sacred picture of Saint Anthony alone is one vertical, unwavering band of light. If a cockroach were near him, or a cocktail waitress, the picture would show two such bands of light. Our awareness is all that is alive and maybe sacred in any of us. Everything else about us is dead machinery.

"I have just heard from this cocktail waitress here, this vertical band of light, a story about her husband and an idiot who was about to be executed at Shepherdstown. Very well—

let a five-year-old paint a sacred interpretation of that encounter. Let that five-year-old strip away the idiocy, the bars, the waiting electric chair, the uniform of the guard, the gun of the guard, the bones and meat of the guard. What is that perfect picture which any five-year-old can paint? Two unwavering bands of light."

Ecstasy bloomed on the barbaric face of Rabo Karabekian. "Citizens of Midland City, I salute you," he said. "You have given a home to a masterpiece!"

Dwayne Hoover, incidentally, wasn't taking any of this in. He was still hypnotized, turned inward. He was thinking about moving fingers writing and moving on, and so forth. He had bats in his bell tower. He was off his rocker. He wasn't playing with a full deck of cards.

20

WHILE MY LIFE was being renewed by the words of Rabo Karabekian, Kilgore Trout found himself standing on the shoulder of the Interstate, gazing across Sugar Creek in its concrete trough at the new Holiday Inn. There were no bridges across the creek. He would have to wade.

So he sat down on a guardrail, removed his shoes and socks, rolled his pantlegs to his knees. His bared shins were rococo with varicose veins and scars. So were the shins of my father when he was an old, old man.

Kilgore Trout had my father's shins. They were a present from me. I gave him my father's feet, too, which were long and narrow and sensitive. They were azure. They were artistic feet.

.   .   .

Trout lowered his artistic feet into the concrete trough containing Sugar Creek. They were coated at once with a clear plastic substance from the surface of the creek. When, in some surprise, Trout lifted one coated foot from the water, the plastic substance dried in air instantly, sheathed his foot in a thin, skin-tight bootie resembling mother-of-pearl. He repeated the process with his other foot.

The substance was coming from the Barrytron plant. The company was manufacturing a new anti-personnel bomb for the Air Force. The bomb scattered plastic pellets instead of steel pellets, because the plastic pellets were cheaper. They were also impossible to locate in the bodies of wounded enemies by means of x-ray machines.

Barrytron had no idea it was dumping this waste into Sugar Creek. They had hired the Maritimo Brothers Construction Company, which was gangster-controlled, to build a system which would get rid of the waste. They knew the company was gangster-controlled. Everybody knew that. But the Maritimo Brothers were usually the best builders in town. They had built Dwayne Hoover's house, for instance, which was a solid house.

But every so often they would do something amazingly criminal. The Barrytron disposal system was a case in point. It was expensive, and it appeared to be complicated and busy. Actually, though, it was old junk hooked up every which way, concealing a straight run of stolen sewer pipe running directly from Barrytron to Sugar Creek.

Barrytron would be absolutely sick when it learned what a polluter it had become. Throughout its history, it had attempted to be a perfect model of corporate good citizenship, no matter what it cost.

· · ·

Trout now crossed Sugar Creek on my father's legs and feet, and those appendages became more nacreous with every wading stride. He carried his parcels and his shoes and socks on his head, although the water scarcely reached his knee-caps.

He knew how ridiculous he looked. He expected to be received abominably, dreamed of embarrassing the Festival to death. He had come all this distance for an orgy of masochism. He wanted to be treated like a cockroach.

• • •

His situation, insofar as he was a machine, was complex, tragic, and laughable. But the sacred part of him, his awareness, remained an unwavering band of light.

And this book is being written by a meat machine in cooperation with a machine made of metal and plastic. The plastic, incidentally, is a close relative of the gunk in Sugar Creek. And at the core of the writing meat machine is something sacred, which is an unwavering band of light.

At the core of each person who reads this book is a band of unwavering light.

My doorbell has just rung in my New York apartment. And I know what I will find when I open my front door: an unwavering band of light.

God bless Rabo Karabekian!

• • •

Listen: Kilgore Trout climbed out of the trough and onto the asphalt desert which was the parking lot. It was his plan to enter the lobby of the Inn on wet bare feet, to leave footprints on the carpet—like this:

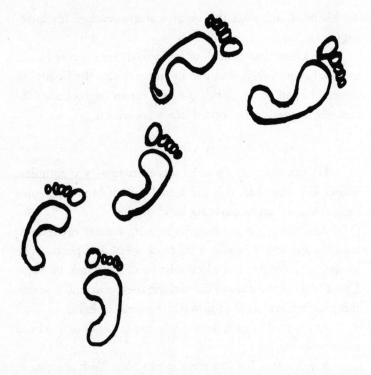

It was Trout's fantasy that somebody would be outraged by the footprints. This would give him the opportunity to reply grandly, "What is it that offends you so? I am simply using man's first printing press. You are reading a bold and universal headline which says, 'I am here, I am here, I am here.'"

• • •

But Trout was no walking printing press. His feet left no marks on the carpet, because they were sheathed in plastic and the plastic was dry. Here was the structure of the plastic molecule:

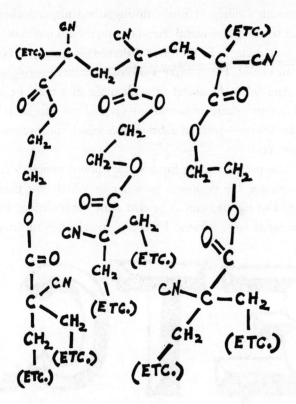

The molecule went on and on and on, repeating itself forever to form a sheet both tough and poreless.

This molecule was the monster Dwayne's twin stepbrothers, Lyle and Kyle, had attacked with their automatic shotguns. This was the same stuff which was fucking up Sacred Miracle Cave.

•   •   •

The man who told me how to diagram a segment of a molecule of plastic was Professor Walter H. Stockmayer of

Dartmouth College. He is a distinguished physical chemist, and an amusing and useful friend of mine. I did not make him up. I would like to be Professor Walter H. Stockmayer. He is a brilliant pianist. He skis like a dream.

And when he sketched a plausible molecule, he indicated points where it would go on and on just as I have indicated them—with an abbreviation which means sameness without end.

The proper ending for any story about people it seems to me, since life is now a polymer in which the Earth is wrapped so tightly, should be that same abbreviation, which I now write large because I feel like it, which is this one:

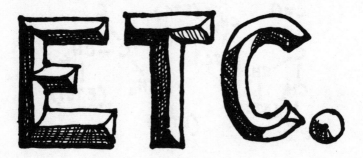

• • •

And it is in order to acknowledge the continuity of this polymer that I begin so many sentences with "And" and "So," and end so many paragraphs with ". . . and so on."

And so on.

"It's all like an ocean!" cried Dostoevski. I say it's all like cellophane.

• • •

So Trout entered the lobby as an inkless printing press, but he was still the most grotesque human being who had ever come in there.

All around him were what other people called *mirrors,* which he called *leaks.* The entire wall which separated the lobby from the cocktail lounge was a *leak* ten feet high and thirty-feet long. There was another *leak* on the cigarette machine and yet another on the candy machine. And when Trout looked through them to see what was going on in the other universe, he saw a red-eyed, filthy old creature who was barefoot, who had his pants rolled up to his knees.

As it happened, the only other person in the lobby at the time was the beautiful young desk clerk, Milo Maritimo. Milo's clothing and skin and eyes were all the colors that olives can be. He was a graduate of the Cornell Hotel School. He was the homosexual grandson of Guillermo "Little Willie" Maritimo, a bodyguard of the notorious Chicago gangster, Al Capone.

Trout presented himself to this harmless man, stood before his desk with his bare feet far apart and his arms outspread. "The Abominable Snowman has arrived," he said to Milo. "If I'm not as clean as most abominable snowmen are, it is because I was kidnapped as a child from the slopes of Mount Everest, and taken as a slave to a bordello in Rio de Janeiro, where I have been cleaning the unspeakably filthy toilets for the past fifty years. A visitor to our whipping room there screamed in a transport of agony and ecstasy that there was to be an arts festival in Midland City. I escaped down a rope of sheets taken from a reeking hamper. I have come to Midland City to have myself acknowledged, before I die, as the great artist I believe myself to be."

Milo Maritimo greeted Trout with luminous adoration.

"Mr. Trout," he said in rapture, "I'd know you anywhere. Welcome to Midland City. We *need* you so!"

"How do you know who I am?" said Kilgore Trout. Nobody had ever known who he was before.

"You *had* to be you," said Milo.

Trout was deflated—*neutralized*. He dropped his arms, became child-like now. "Nobody ever knew who I was before," he said.

"I know," said Milo. "We have discovered you, and we hope you will discover us. No longer will Midland City be known merely as the home of Mary Alice Miller, the Women's Two Hundred Meter Breast Stroke Champion of the World. It will also be the city which first acknowledged the greatness of Kilgore Trout."

Trout simply walked away from the desk and sat down on a brocaded Spanish-style settee. The entire lobby, except for the vending machines, was done in Spanish style.

Milo now used a line from a television show which had been popular a few years back. The show wasn't on the air anymore, but most people still remembered the line. Much of the conversation in the country consisted of lines from television shows, both present and past. The show Milo's line was from consisted of taking some old person, usually fairly famous, into what looked like an ordinary room, only it was actually a stage, with an audience out front and television cameras hidden all around. There were also people who had known the person in the older days hidden around. They would come out and tell anecdotes about the person later on.

Milo now said what the master of ceremonies would have said to Trout, if Trout had been on the show and the curtain was going up: "Kilgore Trout! This is your life!"

. . .

Only there wasn't any audience or curtain or any of that. And the truth was that Milo Maritimo was the only person in Midland City who knew anything about Kilgore Trout. It was wishful thinking on his part that the upper crust of Midland City was about to be as ga-ga as he was about the works of Kilgore Trout.

"We are so ready for a Renaissance, Mr. Trout! You will be our Leonardo!"

"How could you *possibly* have heard of me?" said Trout dazedly.

"In getting ready for the Midland City Renaissance," said Milo, "I made it my business to read everything I could by and about every artist who was on his way here."

"There isn't anything by me or about me anywhere," protested Trout.

Milo came from behind his desk. He brought with him what appeared to be a lopsided old softball, swaddled in many different sorts of tape. "When I couldn't find out anything about you," he said, "I wrote to Eliot Rosewater, the man who said we had to bring you here. He has a private collection of forty-one of your novels and sixty-three of your short stories, Mr. Trout. He let me read them all." He held out the seeming baseball, which was actually a book from Rosewater's collection. Rosewater used his science-fiction library hard. "This is the only book I haven't finished, and I'll finish it before the sun comes up tomorrow," said Milo.

. . .

The novel in question, incidentally, was *The Smart Bunny*. The leading character was a rabbit who lived like all the other wild rabbits, but who was as intelligent as Albert Einstein or William Shakespeare. It was a female rabbit. She was the only female leading character in any novel or story by Kilgore Trout.

She led a normal female rabbit's life, despite her ballooning intellect. She concluded that her mind was useless, that it was a sort of tumor, that it had no usefulness within the rabbit scheme of things.

So she went hippity-hop, hippity-hop toward the city, to have the tumor removed. But a hunter named Dudley Farrow shot and killed her before she got there. Farrow skinned her and took out her guts, but then he and his wife Grace decided that they had better not eat her because of her unusually large head. They thought what she had thought when she was alive—that she must be diseased.

And so on.

• • •

Kilgore Trout had to change into his only other garments, his high school tuxedo and his new evening shirt and all, right away. The lower parts of his rolled-up trousers had become impregnated with the plastic substance from the creek, so he couldn't roll them down again. They were as stiff as flanges on sewer pipes.

So Milo Maritimo showed him to his suite, which was two ordinary Holiday Inn rooms with a door between them open. Trout and every distinguished visitor had a suite, with two color television sets, two tile baths, four double beds equipped with *Magic Fingers*. Magic Fingers were electric vibrators attached to the mattress springs of a bed. If a guest put a quarter into a little box on his bedside table, the Magic Fingers would jiggle his bed.

There were enough flowers in Trout's room for a Catholic gangster's funeral. They were from Fred T. Barry, the Chairman of the Arts Festival, and from the Midland City Association of Women's Clubs, and from the Chamber of Commerce, and on and on.

Trout read a few of the cards on the flowers, and he commented, "The town certainly seems to be getting behind the arts in a great big way."

Milo closed his olive eyes tight, wincing with a tangy agony. "It's *time*. Oh God, Mr. Trout, we were starving for so long, without even knowing what we were hungering for," he said. This young man was not only a descendant of master criminals, he was a close relative of felons operating in Midland City at the present time. The partners in the Maritimo Brothers Construction Company, for instance, were his uncles. Gino Maritimo, Milo's first cousin once removed, was the dope king of the city.

• • •

"Oh, Mr. Trout," nice Milo went on, there in Trout's suite, "teach us to sing and dance and laugh and cry. We've tried to survive so long on money and sex and envy and real estate and football and basketball and automobiles and television and alcohol—on sawdust and broken glass!"

"Open your eyes!" said Trout bitterly. "Do I look like a dancer, a singer, a man of joy?" He was wearing his tuxedo now. It was a size too large for him. He had lost much weight since high school. His pockets were crammed with mothballs. They bulged like saddlebags.

"Open your eyes!" said Trout. "Would a man nourished by beauty look like this? You have nothing but desolation and desperation here, you say? I bring you more of the same!"

"My eyes *are* open," said Milo warmly, "and I see exactly what I *expect* to see. I see a man who is terribly wounded—because he has dared to pass through the fires of truth to the other side, which we have never seen. And then he has come back again—to tell us about the other side."

• • •

And I sat there in the new Holiday Inn, and made it disappear, then appear again, then disappear, then appear again. Actually, there was nothing but a big open field there. A farmer had put it into rye.

It was high time, I thought, for Trout to meet Dwayne Hoover, for Dwayne to run amok.

I knew how this book would end. Dwayne would hurt a lot of people. He would bite off one joint of the right index finger of Kilgore Trout.

And then Trout, with his wound dressed, would walk out into the unfamiliar city. He would meet his Creator, who would explain everything.

21

KILGORE TROUT entered the cocktail lounge. His feet were fiery hot. They were encased not only in shoes and socks, but in clear plastic, too. They could not sweat, they could not breathe.

Rabo Karabekian and Beatrice Keedsler did not see him come in. They were surrounded by new affectionate friends at the piano bar. Karabekian's speech had been splendidly received. Everybody agreed now that Midland City had one of the greatest paintings in the world.

"All you had to do was explain," said Bonnie MacMahon. "I understand now."

"I didn't think there was anything *to* explain," said Carlo Maritino, the builder, wonderingly. "But there was, by God."

Abe Cohen, the jeweler, said to Karabekian, "If artists would explain more, people would like art more. You realize that?"

And so on.

Trout was feeling spooky. He thought maybe a lot of people were going to greet him as effusively as Milo Maritimo had done, and he had had no experience with celebrations like that. But nobody got in his way. His old friend Anonymity was by his side again, and the two of them chose a table near Dwayne Hoover and me. All he could see of me was the reflection of candle flames in my mirrored glasses, in my *leaks*.

Dwayne Hoover was still mentally absent from activities in the cocktail lounge. He sat like a lump of nose putty, staring at something long ago and far away.

Dwayne moved his lips as Trout sat down. He was saying this soundlessly, and it had nothing to do with Trout or me: "Goodbye, Blue Monday."

· · ·

Trout had a fat manila envelope with him. Milo Maritimo had given it to him. It contained a program for the Festival of the Arts, a letter of welcome to Trout from Fred T. Barry, the Chairman of the Festival, a timetable of events during the coming week—and some other things.

Trout also carried a copy of his novel *Now It Can Be Told*. This was the wide-open beaver book which Dwayne Hoover would soon take so seriously.

So there the three of us were. Dwayne and Trout and I could have been included in an equilateral triangle about twelve feet on a side.

As three unwavering bands of light, we were simple and separate and beautiful. As machines, we were flabby bags of ancient plumbing and wiring, of rusty hinges and feeble springs. And our interrelationships were Byzantine.

After all, I had created both Dwayne and Trout, and now Trout was about to drive Dwayne into full-blown insanity, and Dwayne would soon bite off the tip of Trout's finger.

· · ·

Wayne Hoobler was watching us through a peephole in the kitchen. There was a tap on his shoulder. The man who had fed him now told him to leave.

So he wandered outdoors, and he found himself among Dwayne's used cars again. He resumed his conversation with the traffic on the Interstate.

• • •

The bartender in the cocktail lounge now flicked on the ultraviolet lights in the ceiling. Bonnie MacMahon's uniform, since it was impregnated with fluorescent materials, lit up like an electric sign.

So did the bartender's jacket and the African masks on the walls.

So did Dwayne Hoover's shirt, and the shirts of several other men. The reason was this: Those shirts had been laundered in washday products which contained fluorescent materials. The idea was to make clothes look brighter in sunlight by making them actually fluorescent.

When the same clothes were viewed in a dark room under ultraviolet light, however, they became ridiculously bright.

Bunny Hoover's teeth also lit up, since he used a toothpaste containing fluorescent materials, which was supposed to make his smile look brighter in daylight. He grinned now, and he appeared to have a mouthful of little Christmas tree lights.

But the brightest new light in the room by far was the bosom of Kilgore Trout's new evening shirt. Its brilliance twinkled and had depth. It might have been the top of a slumping, open sack of radioactive diamonds.

But then Trout hunched forward involuntarily, buckling

the starched shirt bosom, forming it into a parabolic dish. This made a searchlight of the shirt. Its beam was aimed at Dwayne Hoover.

The sudden light roused Dwayne from his trance. He thought perhaps he had died. At any rate, something painless and supernatural was going on. Dwayne smiled trustingly at the holy light. He was ready for anything.

• • •

Trout had no explanation for the fantastic transformation of certain garments around the room. Like most science-fiction writers, he knew almost nothing about science. He had no more use for solid information than did Rabo Karabekian. So now he could only be flabbergasted.

My own shirt, being an old one which had been washed many times in a Chinese laundry which used ordinary soap, did not fluoresce.

Dwayne Hoover now lost himself in the bosom of Trout's shirt, just as he had earlier lost himself in twinkling beads of lemon oil. He remembered now a thing his stepfather had told him when he was only ten years old, which was this: Why there were no Niggers in Shepherdstown.

This was not a completely irrelevant recollection. Dwayne had, after all, been talking to Bonnie MacMahon, whose husband had lost so much money in a car wash in Shepherdstown. And the main reason the car wash had failed was that successful car washes needed cheap and plentiful labor, which meant black labor—and there were no Niggers in Shepherdstown.

"Years ago," Dwayne's stepfather told Dwayne when Dwayne was ten, "Niggers was coming up north by the millions—to Chicago, to Midland City, to Indianapolis, to Detroit. The World War was going on. There was such a labor shortage that even Niggers who couldn't read or write could get good factory jobs. Niggers had money like they never had before.

"Over at Shepherdstown, though," he went on, "the white people got smart quick. They didn't want Niggers in their town, so they put up signs on the main roads at the city limits and in the railroad yard." Dwayne's stepfather described the signs, which looked like this:

"One night—" Dwayne's stepfather said, "a Nigger family got off a boxcar in Shepherdstown. Maybe they didn't see the sign. Maybe they couldn't read it. Maybe they couldn't believe it." Dwayne's stepfather was out of work when he told the story so gleefully. The Great Depression had just begun. He and Dwayne were on a weekly expedition in the family car, hauling garbage and trash out into the country, where they dumped it all in Sugar Creek.

"Anyway, they moved into an empty shack that night," Dwayne's stepfather went on. "They got a fire going in the stove and all. So a mob went down there at midnight. They took out the man, and they sawed him in two on the top strand of a barbed-wire fence." Dwayne remembered clearly that a rainbow of oil from the trash was spreading prettily over the surface of Sugar Creek when he heard that.

"Since that night, which was a long time ago now," his stepfather said, "there ain't been a Nigger even spend the night in Shepherdstown.

• • •

Trout was itchingly aware that Dwayne was staring at his bosom so loonily. Dwayne's eyes swam, and Trout supposed they were swimming in alcohol. He could not know that Dwayne was seeing an oil slick on Sugar Creek which had made rainbows forty long years ago.

Trout was aware of me, too, what little he could see of me. I made him even more uneasy than Dwayne did. The thing was: Trout was the only character I ever created who had enough imagination to suspect that he might be the creation of another human being. He had spoken of this possibility several times to his parakeet. He had said, for instance, "Honest to God, Bill, the way things are going, all I can think of is that I'm a character in a book by somebody who wants to write about somebody who suffers all the time."

Now Trout was beginning to catch on that he was sitting very close to the person who had created him. He was embarrassed. It was hard for him to know how to respond, particularly since his responses were going to be anything I said they were.

I went easy on him, didn't wave, didn't stare. I kept my glasses on. I wrote again on my tabletop, scrawled the symbols for the interrelationship between matter and energy as it was understood in my day:

$$E = Mc^2$$

It was a flawed equation, as far as I was concerned. There should have been an "A" in there somewhere for *Awareness*—without which the "E" and the "M" and the "c," which was a mathematical constant; could not exist.

. . .

All of us were stuck to the surface of a ball, incidentally. The planet was ball-shaped. Nobody knew why we didn't fall off, even though everybody pretended to kind of understand it.

The really smart people understood that one of the best ways to get rich was to own a part of the surface people had to stick to.

• • •

Trout dreaded eye contact with either Dwayne or me, so he went through the contents of the manila envelope which had been waiting for him in his suite.

The first thing he examined was a letter from Fred T. Barry, the Chairman of the Festival of the Arts, the donor of the Mildred Barry Memorial Center for the Arts, and the founder and Chairman of the Board of Directors of Barry-tron, Ltd.

Clipped to the letter was one share of common stock in Barrytron, made out in the name of Kilgore Trout. Here was the letter:

"Dear Mr. Trout:" it said, "It is a pleasure and an honor to have such a distinguished and creative person give his precious time to Midland City's first Festival of the Arts. It is our wish that you feel like a member of our family while you are here. To give you and other distinguished visitors a deeper sense of participation in the life of our community, I am making a gift to each of you of one share in the company which I founded, the company of which I am now Chairman of the Board. It is not only my company now, but yours as well.

"Our company began as The Robo-Magic Corporation of America in 1934. It had three employees in the beginning, and its mission was to design and manufacture the first fully automatic washing machine for use in the home. You will find the motto of that washing machine on the corporate emblem at the top of the stock certificate."

The emblem consisted of a Greek goddess on an ornate chaise longue. She held a flagstaff from which a long pennant streamed. Here is what the pennant said:

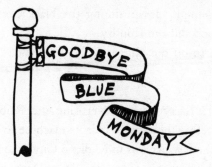

. . .

The motto of the old Robo-Magic washing machine cleverly confused two separate ideas people had about Monday. One idea was that women traditionally did their laundry on Monday. Monday was simply washday, and not an especially depressing day on that account.

People who had horrible jobs during the week used to call Monday "Blue Monday" sometimes, though, because they hated to return to work after a day of rest. When Fred T. Barry made up the Robo-Magic motto as a young man, he pretended that Monday was called "Blue Monday" because doing the laundry disgusted and exhausted women.

The Robo-Magic was going to cheer them up.

. . .

It wasn't true, incidentally, that most women did their laundry on Monday at the time the Robo-Magic was invented. They did it any time they felt like it. One of Dwayne Hoover's clearest recollections from the Great Depression, for instance, was when his stepmother decided to do the laundry on Christmas Eve. She was bitter about the low estate to which the family had fallen, and she suddenly clumped down into the basement, down among the black beetles and the millipedes, and did the laundry.

"Time to do the Nigger work," she said.

• • •

Fred T. Barry began advertising the Robo-Magic in 1933, long before there was a reliable machine to sell. And he was one of the few persons in Midland City who could afford billboard advertising during the Great Depression, so the Robo-Magic sales message did not have to jostle and shriek for attention. It was practically the only symbol in town.

One of Fred's ads was on a billboard outside the main gate of the defunct Keedsler Automobile Company, which the Robo-Magic Corporation had taken over. It showed a high society woman in a fur coat and pearls. She was leaving her mansion for a pleasant afternoon of idleness, and a balloon was coming out of her mouth. These were the words in the balloon:

OFF TO THE BRIDGE CLUB WHILE MY ROBO-MAGIC DOES THE WASH! GOODBYE, BLUE MONDAY!

Another ad, which was painted on a billboard by the railroad depot, showed two white deliverymen who were bringing a Robo-Magic into a house. A black maid was watching them. Her eyes were popping out in a comical way. There was a balloon coming out of her mouth, too, and she was saying this:

FEETS, GET MOVIN'! DEY'S GOT THEIRSELVES A ROBO-MAGIC! DEY AIN'T GONNA BE NEEDIN' US 'ROUN' HERE NO MO'!

* * *

Fred T. Barry wrote these ads himself, and he predicted at the time that Robo-Magic appliances of various sorts would eventually do what he called "all the Nigger work of the world," which was lifting and cleaning and cooking and washing and ironing and tending children and dealing with filth.

Dwayne Hoover's stepmother wasn't the only white woman who was a terrible sport about doing work like that. My own mother was that way, too, and so was my sister, may she rest in peace. They both flatly refused to do Nigger work.

The white men wouldn't do it either, of course. They called it *women's work,* and the women called it *Nigger work.*

* * *

I am going to make a wild guess now: I think that the end of the Civil War in my country frustrated the white people in the North, who won it, in a way which has never been

251

acknowledged before. Their descendants inherited that frustration, I think, without ever knowing what it was.

The victors in that war were cheated out of the most desirable spoils of that war, which were human slaves.

• • •

The Robo-Magic dream was interrupted by World War Two. The old Keedsler Automobile Works became an armory instead of an appliance factory. All that survived of the Robo-Magic itself was its brain, which had told the rest of the machine when to let the water in, when to let the water out, when to slosh, when to rinse, when to spin dry, and so on.

That brain became the nerve center of the so-called "BLINC System" during the Second World War. It was installed on heavy bombers, and it did the actual dropping of bombs after a bombardier pressed his bright red "bombs away" button. The button activated the BLINC System, which then released the bombs in such a way as to achieve a desired pattern of explosions on the planet below. "BLINC" was an abbreviation of "Blast Interval Normalization Computer."

22

AND I SAT THERE in the cocktail lounge of the new Holiday Inn, watching Dwayne Hoover stare into the bosom of the shirt of Kilgore Trout. I was wearing a bracelet which looked like this:

WO1 stood for Warrant Officer First Class, which was the rank of Jon Sparks.

The bracelet had cost me two dollars and a half. It was a way of expressing my pity for the hundreds of Americans who had been taken prisoner during the war in Viet Nam. Such bracelets were becoming popular. Each one bore the name of an actual prisoner of war, his rank, and the date of his capture.

Wearers of the bracelets weren't supposed to take them off until the prisoners came home or were reported dead or missing.

I wondered how I might fit my bracelet into my story, and hit on the good idea of dropping it somewhere for Wayne Hoobler to find.

Wayne would assume that it belonged to a woman who loved somebody named WO1 Jon Sparks, and that the woman and WO1 had become engaged or married or something important on March 19th, 1971.

Wayne would mouth the unusual first name tentatively. "Woo-*ee*?" he would say. "*Woe*-ee? *Woe*-eye? Woy?"

• • •

There in the cocktail lounge, I gave Dwayne Hoover credit for having taken a course in speed-reading at night at the Young Men's Christian Association. This would enable him to read Kilgore Trout's novel in minutes instead of hours.

• • •

There in the cocktail lounge, I took a white pill which a doctor said I could take in moderation, two a day, in order not to feel blue.

• • •

There in the cocktail lounge, the pill and the alcohol gave me a terrific sense of urgency about explaining all the things I hadn't explained yet, and then hurtling on with my tale.

Let's see: I have already explained Dwayne's uncharacteristic ability to read so fast. Kilgore Trout probably couldn't have made his trip from New York City in the time I allotted, but it's too late to bugger around with that. Let it stand, let it stand!

Let's see, let's see. Oh, yes—I have to explain a jacket Trout will see at the hospital. It will look like this from the back:

Here is the explanation: There used to be only one Nigger high school in Midland City, and it was an all-Nigger high school still. It was named after Crispus Attucks, a black man who was shot by British troops in Boston in 1770. There was an oil painting of this event in the main corridor of the school. Several white people were stopping bullets, too. Crispus Attucks himself had a hole in his forehead which looked like the front door of a birdhouse.

But the black people didn't call the school *Crispus Attucks High School* anymore. They called it *Innocent Bystander High*.

And when another Nigger high school was built after the Second World War, it was named after George Washington Carver, a black man who was born into slavery, but who became a famous chemist anyway. He discovered many remarkable new uses for peanuts.

But the black people wouldn't call that school by its proper name, either. On the day it opened, there were already young black people wearing jackets which looked like this from the back:

• • •

I have to explain, too, see, why so many black people in Midland City were able to imitate birds from various parts of what used to be the British Empire. The thing was, see, that Fred T. Barry and his mother and father were almost the only people in Midland City who could afford to hire Niggers to do the Nigger work during the Great Depression. They took over the old Keedsler Mansion, where Beatrice Keedsler, the novelist, had been born. They had as many as twenty servants working there, all at one time.

Fred's father got so much money during the prosperity of the twenties as a bootlegger and as a swindler in stocks and bonds. He kept all his money in cash, which turned out to be a bright thing to do, since so many banks failed during the Great Depression. Also: Fred's father was an agent for Chicago gangsters who wanted to buy legitimate businesses for their children and grandchildren. Through Fred's father, those gangsters bought almost every desirable property in Midland City for anything from a tenth to a hundredth of what it was really worth.

And before Fred's mother and father came to the United States after the First World War, they were music hall entertainers in England. Fred's father played the musical saw. His mother imitated birds from various parts of what was still the British Empire.

She went on imitating them for her own amusement, well into the Great Depression. "The Bulbul of Malaysia," she would say, for instance, and then she would imitate that bird.

"The Morepark Owl of New Zealand," she would say, and then she would imitate that bird.

And all the black people who worked for her thought her act was the funniest thing they had ever seen, though they never laughed out loud when she did it. And, in order to double up their friends and relatives with laughter, they, too, learned how to imitate the birds.

The craze spread. Black people who had never been near the Keedsler mansion could imitate the Lyre Bird and the Willy Wagtail of Australia, the Golden Oriole of India, the

Nightingale and the Chaffinch and the Wren and the Chiffchaff of England itself.

They could even imitate the happy screech of the extinct companion of Kilgore Trout's island childhood, which was the Bermuda Ern.

When Kilgore Trout hit town, the black people could still imitate those birds, and say word for word what Fred's mother had said before each imitation. If one of them imitated a Nightingale, for instance, he or she would say this first: "What adds peculiar beauty to the call of the Nightingale, much beloved by poets, is the fact that it will *only* sing by moonlight."

And so on.

• • •

There in the cocktail lounge, Dwayne Hoover's bad chemicals suddenly decided that it was time for Dwayne to demand from Kilgore Trout the secrets of life.

"Give me the message," cried Dwayne. He tottered up from his own banquette, crashed down again next to Trout, throwing off heat like a steam radiator. "The message, please."

And here Dwayne did something extraordinarily unnatural. He did it because I wanted him to. It was something I had ached to have a character do for years and years. Dwayne did to Trout what the Duchess did to Alice in Lewis Carroll's *Alice's Adventures in Wonderland*. He rested his chin on poor Trout's shoulder, dug in with his chin.

"The message?" he said, digging in his chin, digging in his chin.

Trout made no reply. He had hoped to get through what little remained of his life without ever having to touch another human being again. Dwayne's chin on his shoulder was as shattering as buggery to Trout.

"Is this it? Is this it?" said Dwayne, snatching up Trout's novel, *Now It Can Be Told*.

"Yes—that's it," croaked Trout. To his tremendous relief, Dwayne removed his chin from his shoulder.

Dwayne now began to read hungrily, as though starved for print. And the speed-reading course he had taken at the Young Men's Christian Association allowed him to make a perfect pig of himself with pages and words.

"Dear Sir, poor sir, brave sir:" he read, "You are an experiment by the Creator of the Universe. You are the only creature in the entire Universe who has free will. You are the only one who has to figure out what to do next—and *why*. Everybody else is a robot, a machine.

"Some persons seem to like you, and others seem to hate you, and you must wonder why. They are simply liking machines and hating machines.

"You are pooped and demoralized," read Dwayne. "Why wouldn't you be? Of course it is exhausting, having to reason all the time in a universe which wasn't meant to be reasonable."

23

DWAYNE HOOVER read on: "You are surrounded by loving machines, hating machines, greedy machines, unselfish machines, brave machines, cowardly machines, truthful machines, lying machines, funny machines, solemn machines," he read. "Their only purpose is to stir you up in every conceivable way, so the Creator of the Universe can watch your reactions. They can no more feel or reason than grandfather clocks.

"The Creator of the Universe would now like to apologize not only for the capricious, jostling companionship he provided during the test, but for the trashy, stinking condition of the planet itself. The Creator programmed robots to abuse it for millions of years, so it would be a poisonous, festering cheese when you got here. Also, He made sure it would be desperately crowded by programming robots, regardless of their living conditions, to crave sexual intercourse and adore infants more than almost anything."

. . .

Mary Alice Miller, incidentally, the Women's Breast Stroke Champion of the World and Queen of the Arts Festival, now passed through the cocktail lounge. She made a shortcut to the lobby from the side parking lot, where her father was waiting for her in his avocado 1970 Plymouth *Barracuda* fastback, which he had bought as a used car from Dwayne. It had a new car guarantee.

Mary Alice's father, Don Miller, was, among other things, Chairman of the Parole Board at Shepherdstown. It was he who had decided that Wayne Hoobler, lurking among Dwayne's used cars again, was fit to take his place in society.

Mary Alice went into the lobby to get a crown and scepter for her performance as Queen at the Arts Festival banquet that night. Milo Maritimo, the desk clerk, the gangster's grandson, had made them with his own two hands. Her eyes were permanently inflamed. They looked like maraschino cherries.

Only one person noticed her sufficiently to comment out loud. He was Abe Cohen, the jeweler. He said this about Mary Alice, despising her sexlessness and innocence and empty mind: "Pure tuna fish!"

• • •

Kilgore Trout heard him say that—about pure tuna fish. His mind tried to make sense of it. His mind was swamped with mysteries. He might as well have been Wayne Hoobler, adrift among Dwayne's used cars during Hawaiian Week.

His feet, which were sheathed in plastic, were meanwhile getting hotter all the time. The heat was painful now. His feet were curling and twisting, begging to be plunged into cold water or waved in the air.

And Dwayne read on about himself and the Creator of the Universe, to wit:

"He also programmed robots to write books and magazines and newspapers for you, and television and radio shows, and stage shows, and films. They wrote songs for you. The Creator of the Universe had them invent hundreds of religions, so you would have plenty to choose among. He had them kill each other by the millions, for this purpose only: that you be amazed. They have committed every possible atrocity and every possible kindness unfeelingly, automatically, inevitably, to get a reaction from Y-O-U."

This last word was set in extra-large type and had a line all to itself, so it looked like this:

"Every time you went into the library," said the book, "the Creator of the Universe held His breath. With such a higgledy-piggledy cultural smorgasbord before you, what would you, with your free will, choose?"

"Your parents were fighting machines and self-pitying machines," said the book. "Your mother was programmed to bawl out your father for being a defective moneymaking machine, and your father was programmed to bawl her out for being a defective housekeeping machine. They were programmed to bawl each other out for being defective loving machines.

"Then your father was programmed to stomp out of the house and slam the door. This automatically turned your mother into a weeping machine. And your father would go down to a tavern where he would get drunk with some other drinking machines. Then all the drinking machines would go to a whorehouse and rent fucking machines. And then your father would drag himself home to become an apologizing machine. And your mother would become a very slow forgiving machine."

• • •

Dwayne got to his feet now, having wolfed down tens of thousands of words of such solipsistic whimsey in ten minutes or so.

He walked stiffly over to the piano bar. What made him stiff was his awe of his own strength and righteousness. He dared not use his full strength in merely walking, for fear of destroying the new Holiday Inn with footfalls. He did not fear for his own life, Trout's book assured him that he had already been killed twenty-three times. On each occasion, the Creator of the Universe had patched him up and got him going again.

Dwayne restrained himself in the name of elegance rather than safety. He was going to respond to his new understanding of life with finesse, for an audience of two—himself and his Creator.

He approached his homosexual son.

Bunny saw the trouble coming, supposed it was death. He might have protected himself easily with all the techniques of fighting he had learned in military school. But he chose to meditate instead. He closed his eyes, and his awareness sank into the silence of the unused lobes of his mind. This phosphorescent scarf floated by:

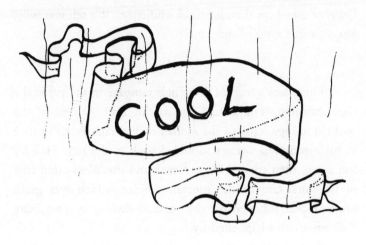

• • •

Dwayne shoved Bunny's head from behind. He rolled it like a cantaloupe up and down the keys of the piano bar. Dwayne laughed, and he called his son ". . . a God damn cock-sucking machine!"

Bunny did not resist him, even though Bunny's face was being mangled horribly. Dwayne hauled his head from the keys, slammed it down again. There was blood on the keys—and spit, and mucus.

Rabo Karabekian and Beatrice Keedsler and Bonnie MacMahon all grabbed Dwayne now, pulled him away from Bunny. This increased Dwayne's glee. "Never hit a woman, right?" he said to the Creator of the Universe.

He then socked Beatrice Keedsler on the jaw. He

punched Bonnie MacMahon in the belly. He honestly believed that they were unfeeling machines.

"All you robots want to know why my wife ate Drāno?" Dwayne asked his thunderstruck audience. "I'll tell you why: She was that kind of machine!"

• • •

There was a map of Dwayne's rampage in the paper the next morning. The dotted line of his route started in the cocktail lounge, crossed the asphalt to Francine Pefko's office in his automobile agency, doubled back to the new Holiday Inn again, then crossed Sugar Creek and the Westbound lane of the Interstate to the median divider, which was grass. Dwayne was subdued on the median divider by two State Policemen who happened by.

Here is what Dwayne said to the policemen as they cuffed his hands behind his back: "Thank God you're here!"

• • •

Dwayne didn't kill anybody on his rampage, but he hurt eleven people so badly they had to go to the hospital. And on the map in the newspaper there was a mark indicating each place where a person had been injured seriously. This was the mark, greatly enlarged:

• • •

In the newspaper map of Dwayne's rampage, there were three such crosses inside the cocktail lounge—for Bunny and Beatrice Keedsler and Bonnie MacMahon.

Then Dwayne ran out onto the asphalt between the Inn and his used car lot. He yelled for Niggers out there, telling them to come at once. "I want to talk to you," he said.

He was out there all alone. Nobody from the cocktail lounge had followed him yet. Mary Alice Miller's father, Don Miller, was in his car near Dwayne, waiting for Mary Alice to come back with her crown and scepter, but he never saw anything of the show Dwayne put on. His car had seats whose backs could be made to lie flat. They could be made into beds. Don was lying on his back, with his head well below window level, resting, staring at the ceiling. He was trying to learn French by means of listening to lessons recorded on tape.

"Demain nous allons passer la soirée au cinéma," said the tape, and Don tried to say it, too. "Nous espérons que notre grand-père vivra encore longtemps," said the tape. And so on.

• • •

Dwayne went on calling for Niggers to come talk to him. He smiled. He thought that the Creator of the Universe had programmed them all to hide, as a joke.

Dwayne glanced around craftily. Then he called out a signal he had used as a child to indicate that a game of hide-and-seek was over, that it was time for children in hiding to go home.

Here is what he called, and the sun was down when he called it: "Olly-olly-ox-in-freeeeeeeeeeeeeeeeeeeeeeeeeeeeee."

The person who answered this incantation was a person who had never played hide-and-seek in his life. It was Wayne Hoobler, who came out from among the used cars quietly. He clasped his hands behind his back and placed his feet apart. He assumed the position known as *parade rest*. This position was taught to soldiers and prisoners alike—as a way of demonstrating attentiveness, gullibility, respect, and voluntary defenselessness. He was ready for anything, and wouldn't mind death.

"There you are," said Dwayne, and his eyes crinkled in bittersweet amusement. He didn't know who Wayne was. He welcomed him as a typical black robot. Any other black robot would have served as well. And Dwayne again carried on a wry talk with the Creator of the Universe, using a robot as an unfeeling conversation piece. A lot of people in Midland City put useless objects from Hawaii or Mexico or someplace like that on their coffee tables or their livingroom end tables or on what-not shelves—and such an object was called a *conversation piece*.

Wayne remained at parade rest while Dwayne told of his year as a County Executive for the Boy Scouts of America, when more black young people were brought into scouting than in any previous year. Dwayne told Wayne about his efforts to save the life of a young black man named Payton Brown, who, at the age of fifteen and a half, became the youngest person ever to die in the electric chair at Shepherdstown. Dwayne rambled on about all the black people he had hired when nobody else would hire black people, about how they never seemed to be able to get to work on time. He mentioned a few, too, who had been energetic and punctual, and he winked at Wayne, and he said this: "They were programmed that way."

He spoke of his wife and son again, acknowledged that

white robots were just like black robots, essentially, in that they were programmed to be whatever they were, to do whatever they did.

Dwayne was silent for a moment after that.

Mary Alice Miller's father was meanwhile continuing to learn conversational French while lying down in his automobile, only a few yards away.

And then Dwayne took a swing at Wayne. He meant to slap him hard with his open hand, but Wayne was very good at ducking. He dropped to his knees as the hand swished through the air where his face had been.

Dwayne laughed. "African dodger!" he said. This had reference to a sort of carnival booth which was popular when Dwayne was a boy. A black man would stick his head through a hole in a piece of canvas at the back of a booth, and people would pay money for the privilege of throwing hard baseballs at his head. If they hit his head, they won a prize.

• • •

So Dwayne thought that the Creator of the Universe had invited him to play a game of African dodger now. He became cunning, concealed his violent intentions with apparent boredom. Then he kicked at Wayne very suddenly.

Wayne dodged again, and had to dodge yet again almost instantly, as Dwayne advanced with quick combinations of intended kicks, slaps, and punches. And Wayne vaulted onto the bed of a very unusual truck, which had been built on the chassis of a 1962 Cadillac limousine. It had belonged to the Maritimo Brothers Construction Company.

Wayne's new elevation gave him a view past Dwayne of both barrels of the Interstate, and of a mile or more of Will Fairchild Memorial Airport, which lay beyond. And it is important to understand at this point that Wayne had never seen an airport before, was unprepared for what could happen to an airport when a plane came in at night.

"That's all right, that's all right," Dwayne assured Wayne. He was being a very good sport. He had no intention of climbing up on the truck for another swing at Wayne. He was winded, for one thing. For another, he understood that Wayne was a perfect dodging machine. Only a perfect hitting machine could hit him. "You're too good for me," said Dwayne.

So Dwayne backed away some, contented himself with preaching up at Wayne. He spoke about human slavery—not only black slaves, but white slaves, too. Dwayne regarded coal miners and workers on assembly lines and so forth as slaves, no matter what color they were. "I used to think that was such a shame," he said. "I used to think the electric chair was a shame. I used to think war was a shame—and automobile accidents and cancer," he said, and so on.

He didn't think they were shames anymore. "Why should I care what happens to machines?" he said.

Wayne Hoobler's face had been blank so far, but now it began to bloom with uncontrollable awe. His mouth fell open.

The runaway lights of Will Fairchild Memorial Airport had just come on. Those lights looked like miles and miles of bewilderingly beautiful jewelry to Wayne. He was seeing a dream come true on the other side of the Interstate.

The inside of Wayne's head lit up in recognition of that dream, lit up with an electric sign which gave a childish name to the dream—like this:

24

Listen: Dwayne Hoover hurt so many people seriously that a special ambulance known as *Martha* was called, *Martha* was a full-sized General Motors transcontinental bus, but with the seats removed. There were beds for thirty-six disaster victims in there, plus a kitchen and a bathroom and an operating room. It had enough food and medical supplies aboard to serve as an independent little hospital for a week without help from the outside world.

Its full name was *The Martha Simmons Memorial Mobile Disaster Unit,* named in honor of the wife of Newbolt Simmons, a County Commissioner of Public Safety. She had died of rabies contracted from a sick bat she found clinging to her floor-to-ceiling livingroom draperies one morning. She had just been reading a biography of Albert Schweitzer, who believed that human beings should treat simpler animals lovingly. The bat nipped her ever so slightly as she wrapped it in *Kleenex,* a face tissue. She carried it out onto her patio, where she laid it gently on a form of artificial grass known as *Astroturf.*

She had thirty-six-inch hips, a twenty-nine-inch waist, and a thirty-eight-inch bosom at the time of her death. Her husband had a penis seven and a half inches long and two inches in diameter.

He and Dwayne were drawn together for a while—because his wife and Dwayne's wife had died such strange deaths within a month of each other.

They bought a gravel pit together, out on Route 23A, but then the Maritimo Brothers Construction Company offered them twice what they had paid for it. So they accepted the offer and divided up the profits, and the friendship petered out somehow. They still exchanged Christmas cards.

Dwayne's most recent Christmas card to Newbolt Simmons looked like this:

Newbolt Simmons' most recent Christmas card to Dwayne looked like this:

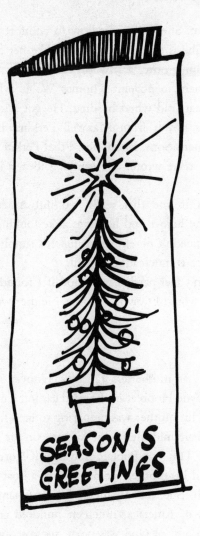

. . .

My psychiatrist is also named Martha. She gathers jumpy
people together into little families which meet once a week.

It's a lot of fun. She teaches us how to comfort one another intelligently. She is on vacation now. I like her a lot.

And I think now, as my fiftieth birthday draws near, about the American novelist Thomas Wolfe, who was only thirty-eight years old when he died. He got a lot of help in organizing his novels from Maxwell Perkins, his editor at Charles Scribner's Sons. I have heard that Perkins told him to keep in mind as he wrote, as a unifying idea, a hero's search for a father.

It seems to me that really truthful American novels would have the heroes and heroines alike looking for *mothers* instead. This needn't be embarrassing. It's simply true.

A mother is much more useful.

I wouldn't feel particularly good if I found another father. Neither would Dwayne Hoover. Neither would Kilgore Trout.

●   ●   ●

And just as motherless Dwayne Hoover was berating motherless Wayne Hoobler in the used car lot, a man who had actually killed his mother was preparing to land in a chartered plane at Will Fairchild Memorial Airport, on the other side of the Interstate. This was Eliot Rosewater, Kilgore Trout's patron. He killed his mother accidentally in a boating accident, when a youth. She was Women's Chess Champion of the United States of America, nineteen hundred and thirty-six years after the Son of God was born, supposedly. Rosewater killed her the year after that.

It was his pilot who caused the airport's runways to become an ex-convict's idea of fairyland. Rosewater remembered his mother's jewelry when the lights came on. He looked to the west, and he smiled at the rosy loveliness of the

Mildred Barry Memorial Arts Center, a harvest moon on stilts in a bend of Sugar Creek. It reminded him of how his mother had looked when he saw her through the bleary eyes of infancy.

• • •

I had made him up, of course—and his pilot, too. I put Colonel Looseleaf Harper, the man who had dropped an atomic bomb on Nagasaki, Japan, at the controls.

I made Rosewater an alcoholic in another book. I now had him reasonably well sobered up, with the help of Alcoholics Anonymous. I had him use his new-found sobriety, to explore, among other things, the supposed spiritual and physical benefits of sexual orgies with strangers in New York City. He was only confused so far.

I could have killed him, and his pilot, too, but I let them live on. So their plane touched down uneventfully.

• • •

The two physicians on the disaster vehicle named *Martha* were Cyprian Ukwende, of Nigeria, and Khashdrahr Miasma, from the infant nation of Bangladesh. Both were parts of the world which were famous from time to time for having the food run out. Both places were specifically mentioned, in fact, in *Now It Can Be Told,* by Kilgore Trout. Dwayne Hoover read in that book that robots all over the world were constantly running out of fuel and dropping dead, while waiting around to test the only free-willed creature in the Universe, on the off-chance that he should appear.

• • •

At the wheel of the ambulance was Eddie Key, a young black man who was a direct descendant of Francis Scott Key, the white American patriot who wrote the National Anthem. Eddie knew he was descended from Key. He could name more than six hundred of his ancestors, and had at least an anecdote about each. They were Africans, Indians and white men.

He knew, for instance, that his mother's side of the family had once owned the farm on which Sacred Miracle Cave was discovered, that his ancestors had called it "Bluebird Farm."

• • •

Here was why there were so many young foreign doctors on the hospital staff, incidentally: The country didn't produce nearly enough doctors for all the sick people it had, but it had an awful lot of money. So it bought doctors from other countries which didn't have much money.

• • •

Eddie Key knew so much about his ancestry because the black part of his family had done what so many African families still do in Africa, which was to have one member of each generation whose duty it was to memorize the history of the family so far. Eddie Key had begun to store in his mind the names and adventures of ancestors on both his mother's and father's sides of his family when he was only six years old. As he sat in the front of the disaster vehicle, looking out through the windshield, he had the feeling that he himself was a vehicle, and that his eyes were windshields through which his progenitors could look, if they wished to.

Francis Scott Key was only one of thousands back there.

On the off-chance that Key might now be having a look at what had become of the United States of America so far, Eddie focussed his eyes on an American flag which was stuck to the windshield. He said this very quietly: "Still wavin', man."

· · ·

Eddie Key's familiarity with a teeming past made life much more interesting to him than it was to Dwayne, for instance, or to me, or to Kilgore Trout, or to almost any white person in Midland City that day. We had no sense of anybody else using our eyes—or our hands. We didn't even know who our great-grandfathers and great-grandmothers were. Eddie Key was afloat in a river of people who were flowing from here to there in time. Dwayne and Trout and I were pebbles at rest.

And Eddie Key, because he knew so much by heart, was able to have deep, nourishing feelings about Dwayne Hoover, for instance, and about Dr. Cyprian Ukwende, too. Dwayne was a man whose family had taken over Bluebird Farm. Ukwende, an Indaro, was a man whose ancestors had kidnapped an ancestor of Key's on the West Coast of Africa, a man named Ojumwa. The Indaros sold him for a musket to British slave traders, who took him on a sailing ship named the "Skylark" to Charleston, South Carolina, where he was auctioned off as a self-propelled, self-repairing farm machine.

And so on.

· · ·

Dwayne Hoover was now hustled aboard *Martha* through big double doors in her rear, just ahead of the engine compartment. Eddie Key was in the driver's seat, and he watched the action in his rearview mirror. Dwayne was swad-dled so tightly in canvas restraining sheets that his reflection looked to Eddie like a bandaged thumb.

Dwayne didn't notice the restraints. He thought he was on the virgin planet promised by the book by Kilgore Trout. Even when he was laid out horizontally by Cyprian Ukwende and Khashdrahr Miasma, he thought he was standing up. The book had told him that he went swimming in cold water on the virgin planet, that he always yelled something surprising when he climbed out of the icy pool. It was a game. The Creator of the Universe would try to guess what Dwayne would yell each day. And Dwayne would fool him totally.

Here is what Dwayne yelled in the ambulance: "Good-bye, Blue Monday!" Then it seemed to him that another day had passed on the virgin planet, and it was time to yell again. "Not a cough in a carload!" he yelled.

• • •

Kilgore Trout was one of the walking wounded. He was able to climb aboard *Martha* without assistance, and to choose a place to sit where he would be away from real emergencies. He had jumped Dwayne Hoover from behind when Dwayne dragged Francine Pefko out of Dwayne's showroom and onto the asphalt. Dwayne wanted to give her a beating in public, which his bad chemicals made him think she richly deserved.

Dwayne had already broken her jaw and three ribs in the office. When he trundled her outside, there was a fairsize crowd which had drifted out of the cocktail lounge and the kitchen of the new Holiday Inn. "Best fucking machine in the State," he told the crowd. "Wind her up, and she'll fuck you and say she loves you, and she won't shut up till you give her a Colonel Sanders Kentucky Fried Chicken franchise."

And so on. Trout grabbed him from behind.

Trout's right ring finger somehow slipped into Dwayne's mouth, and Dwayne bit off the topmost joint. Dwayne let go of Francine after that, and she slumped to the asphalt. She was unconscious, and the most seriously injured of all. And Dwayne went cantering over to the concrete trough by the Interstate, and he spat Kilgore Trout's fingertip into Sugar Creek.

• • •

Kilgore Trout did not choose to lie down in *Martha*. He settled into a leather bucket seat behind Eddie Key. Key asked him what was the matter with him, and Trout held up his right hand, partly shrouded in a bloody handkerchief, which looked like this:

"A slip of the lip can sink a ship!" yelled Dwayne.

• • •

"Remember Pearl Harbor!" yelled Dwayne. Most of what he had done during the past three-quarters of an hour had been hideously unjust. But he had spared Wayne Hoobler, at least. Wayne was back among the used cars again, unscathed. He was picking up a bracelet which I had pitched back there for him to find.

As for myself: I kept a respectful distance between myself and all the violence—even though I had created Dwayne and his violence and the city, and the sky above and the Earth below. Even so, I came out of the riot with a broken watch crystal and what turned out later to be a broken toe. Somebody jumped backwards to get out of Dwayne's way. He broke my watch crystal, even though I had created him, and he broke my toe.

• • •

This isn't the kind of book where people get what is coming to them at the end. Dwayne hurt only one person who deserved to be hurt for being so wicked: That was Don Breedlove. Breedlove was the white gas-conversion unit installer who had raped Patty Keene, the waitress in Dwayne's Burger Chef out on Crestview Avenue, in the parking lot of George Hickman Bannister Memorial Fieldhouse out at the County Fairgrounds after Peanut University beat Innocent Bystander High School in the Regional Class High School Basketball Playoffs.

• • •

Don Breedlove was in the kitchen of the Inn when Dwayne began his rampage. He was repairing a defective gas oven in there.

He stepped outside for some fresh air, and Dwayne came running up to him. Dwayne had just spit Kilgore Trout's fingertip into Sugar Creek. Don and Dwayne knew each other quite well, since Dwayne had once sold Breedlove a new Pontiac *Ventura,* which Don said was a lemon. A lemon was an automobile which didn't run right, and which nobody was able to repair.

Dwayne actually lost money on the transaction, making adjustments and replacing parts in an attempt to mollify Breedlove. But Breedlove was inconsolable, and he finally painted this sign in bright yellow on his trunk lid and on both doors:

Here was what was really wrong with the car, incidentally. The child of a neighbor of Breedlove had put maple sugar in the gas tank of the *Ventura*. Maple sugar was a kind of candy made from the blood of trees.

So Dwayne Hoover now extended his right hand to Breedlove, and Breedlove without thinking anything about it took that hand in his own. They linked up like this:

This was a symbol of friendship between men. The feeling was, too, that a lot of character could be read into the way a man shook hands. Dwayne and Don Breedlove gave each other squeezes which were dry and hard.

So Dwayne held on to Don Breedlove with his right hand, and he smiled as though bygones were bygones. Then he made a cup out of his left hand, and he hit Don on the ear with the open end of the cup. This created terrific air pressure in Don's ear. He fell down because the pain was so awful. Don would never hear anything with that ear, ever again.

• • •

So Don was in the ambulance, too, now—sitting up like Kilgore Trout. Francine was lying down—unconscious but moaning. Beatrice Keedsler was lying down, although she might have sat up. Her jaw was broken. Bunny Hoover was lying down. His face was unrecognizable, even as a face—

anybody's face. He had been given morphine by Cyprian Ukwende.

There were five other victims as well—one white female, two white males, two black males. The three white people had never been in Midland City before. They were on their way together from Erie, Pennsylvania, to the Grand Canyon, which was the deepest crack on the planet. They wanted to look down into the crack, but they never got to do it. Dwayne Hoover assaulted them as they walked from the car toward the lobby of the New Holiday Inn.

The two black males were both kitchen employees of the Inn.

. . .

Cyprian Ukwende now tried to remove Dwayne Hoover's shoes—but Dwayne's shoes and laces and socks were impregnated with the plastic material, which he had picked up while wading across Sugar Creek.

Ukwende was not mystified by plasticized, unitized shoes and socks. He saw shoes and socks like that every day at the hospital, on the feet of children who had played too close to Sugar Creek. In fact, he had hung a pair of tinsnips on the wall of the hospital's emergency room—for cutting off plasticized, unitized shoes and socks.

He turned to his Bengali assistant, young Dr. Khashdrahr Miasma. "Get some shears," he said.

Miasma was standing with his back to the door of the ladies' toilet on the emergency vehicle. He had done nothing so far to deal with all the emergencies. Ukwende and police and a team from Civil Defense had done the work so far. Miasma now refused even to find some shears.

Basically, Miasma probably shouldn't have been in the

field of medicine at all, or at least not in any area where there was a chance that he might be criticized. He could not tolerate criticism. This was a characteristic beyond his control. Any hint that anything about him was not absolutely splendid automatically turned him into a useless, sulky child who would only say that it wanted to go home.

That was what he said when Ukwende told him a second time to find shears: "I want to go home."

Here is what he had been criticized for, just before the alarm came in about Dwayne's going berserk: He had amputated a black man's foot, whereas the foot could probably have been saved.

And so on.

• • •

I could go on and on with the intimate details about the various lives of people on the super-ambulance, but what good is more information?

I agree with Kilgore Trout about realistic novels and their accumulations of nit-picking details. In Trout's novel, *The Pan-Galactic Memory Bank,* the hero is on a space ship two hundred miles long and sixty-two miles in diameter. He gets a realistic novel out of the branch library in his neighborhood. He reads about sixty pages of it, and then he takes it back.

The librarian asks him why he doesn't like it, and he says to her, "I already know about human beings."

And so on.

• • •

Martha began to move. Kilgore Trout saw a sign he liked a lot. Here is what it said:

And so on.

Dwayne Hoover's awareness returned to Earth momentarily. He spoke of opening a health club in Midland City, with rowing machines and stationary bicycles and whirlpool baths and sunlamps and a swimming pool and so on. He told Cyprian Ukwende that the thing to do with a health club was to open it and then sell it as soon as possible for a profit. "People get all enthusiastic about getting back in shape or losing some pounds," said Dwayne. "They sign up for the program, but then they lose interest in about a year, and they stop coming. That's how people are."

And so on.

Dwayne wasn't going to open any health club. He wasn't going to open anything ever again. The people he had injured so unjustly would sue him so vengefully that he would be rendered destitute. He would become one more withered balloon of an old man on Midland City's Skid Row, which was the neighborhood of the once fashionable Fairchild Hotel. He would be by no means the only drifter of whom it could be truthfully said, "See him? Can you believe it? He doesn't have a doodley-squat now, but he used to be fabulously well-to-do."

And so on.

Kilgore Trout now peeled strips and patches of plastic from his burning shins and feet in the ambulance. He had to use his uninjured left hand.

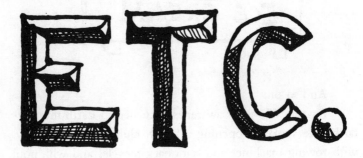

EPILOGUE

THE EMERGENCY ROOM of the hospital was in the basement. After Kilgore Trout had the stump of his ring finger disinfected and trimmed and bandaged, he was told to go upstairs to the finance office. There were certain forms he had to fill out, since he was from outside Midland County, had no health insurance, and was destitute. He had no checkbook. He had no cash.

He got lost in the basement for a little while, as a lot of people did. He found the double doors to the morgue, as a lot of people did. He automatically mooned about his own mortality, as a lot of people did. He found an x-ray room, which wasn't in use. It made him wonder automatically if anything bad was growing inside himself. Other people had wondered exactly the same thing when they passed that room.

Trout felt nothing now that millions of other people wouldn't have felt—automatically.

And Trout found stairs, but they were the wrong stairs. They led him not to the lobby and the finance office and the gift shop and all that, but into a matrix of rooms where persons were recovering or failing to recover from injuries of all kinds. Many of the people there had been flung to the earth by the force of gravity, which never relaxed for a second.

Trout passed a very expensive private room now, and there was a young black man in there, with a white telephone and a color television set and boxes of candy and bouquets of flowers all around. He was Elgin Washington, a pimp who operated out of the old Holiday Inn. He was only twenty-six years old, but he was fabulously well-to-do.

Visiting hours had ended, so all his female sex slaves had departed. But they had left clouds of perfume behind. Trout gagged as he passed the door. It was an automatic reaction to the fundamentally unfriendly cloud. Elgin Washington had just sniffed cocaine into his sinus passages, which amplified tremendously the telepathic messages he sent and received. He felt one hundred times bigger than life, because the messages were so loud and exciting. It was their noise that thrilled him. He didn't care what they said.

And, in the midst of the uproar, Elgin Washington said something wheedlingly to Trout. "Hey man, hey man, hey man," he wheedled. He had had his foot amputated earlier in the day by Khashdrahr Miasma, but he had forgotten that. "Hey man, hey man," he coaxed. He wanted nothing particular from Trout. Some part of his mind was idly exercising his skill at making strangers come to him. He was a fisherman for men's souls. "Hey man—" he said. He showed a gold tooth. He winked an eye.

Trout came to the foot of the black man's bed. This wasn't compassion on his part. He was being machinery again. Trout was, like so many Earthlings, a fully automatic boob when a pathological personality like Elgin Washington told him what to want, what to do. Both men, incidentally, were descendants of the Emperor Charlemagne. Anybody with any European blood in him was a descendant of the Emperor Charlemagne.

Elgin Washington perceived that he had caught yet another human being without really meaning to. It was not in his nature to let one go without making him feel in some way diminished, in some way a fool. Sometimes he actually killed a man in order to diminish him, but he was gentle with Trout. He closed his eyes as though thinking hard, then he earnestly said, "I think I may be dying."

"I'll get a nurse!" said Trout. Any human being would have said exactly the same thing.

"No, no," said Elgin Washington, waving his hands in dreamy protest. "I'm dying *slow*. It's gradual."

"I see," said Trout.

"You got to do me a favor," said Washington. He had no idea what favor to ask. It would come to him. Ideas for favors always came.

"What favor?" said Trout uneasily. He stiffened at the mention of an unspecified favor. He was that kind of a machine. Washington knew he would stiffen. Every human being was that kind of a machine.

"I want you to listen to me while I whistle the song of the Nightingale," he said. He commanded Trout to be silent by giving him the evil eye. "What adds peculiar beauty to the call of the Nightingale, much beloved by poets," he said, "is the fact that it will *only* sing by moonlight." Then he did what almost every black person in Midland City would do: He imitated a Nightingale.

. . .

The Midland City Festival of the Arts was postponed because of madness. Fred T. Barry, its chairman, came to the hospital in his limousine, dressed like a Chinaman, to offer his sympathy to Beatrice Keedsler and Kilgore Trout. Trout could not be found anywhere. Beatrice Keedsler had been put to sleep with morphine.

Kilgore Trout assumed that the Arts Festival would still take place that night. He had no money for any form of transportation, so he set out on foot. He began the five mile walk down Fairchild Boulevard—toward a tiny amber dot at the other end. The dot was the Midland City Center for the Arts. He would make it grow by walking toward it. When his walking had made it big enough, it would swallow him up. There would be food inside.

• • •

I was waiting to intercept him, about six blocks away. I sat in a Plymouth *Duster* I had rented from *Avis* with my *Diners' Club* card, I had a paper tube in my mouth. It was stuffed with leaves. I set it on fire. It was a *soigné* thing to do.

My penis was three inches long and five inches in diameter. Its diameter was a world's record as far as I knew. It slumbered now in my *Jockey Shorts*. And I got out of the car to stretch my legs, which was another soigné thing to do. I was among factories and warehouses. The streetlights were widely-spaced and feeble. Parking lots were vacant, except for night watchmen's cars which were here and there. There was no traffic on Fairchild Boulevard, which had once been the aorta of the town. The life had all been drained out of it by the Interstate and by the Robert F. Kennedy Inner Belt Expressway, which was built on the old right-of-way of the Monon Railroad. The Monon was defunct.

. . .

Defunct.

. . .

Nobody slept in that part of town. Nobody lurked there. It was a system of forts at night, with high fences and alarms, and with prowling dogs. They were killing machines.

When I got out of my Plymouth *Duster,* I feared nothing. That was foolish of me. A writer off-guard, since the materials with which he works are so dangerous, can expect agony as quick as a thunderclap.

I was about to be attacked by a Doberman pinscher. He was a leading character in an earlier version of this book.

. . .

Listen: That Doberman's name was *Kazak.* He patrolled the supply yard of the Maritimo Brothers Construction Company at night. Kazak's trainers, the people who explained to him what sort of a planet he was on and what sort of an animal he was, taught him that the Creator of the Universe wanted him to kill anything he could catch, and to *eat* it, too.

In an earlier version of this book, I had Benjamin Davis, the black husband of Lottie Davis, Dwayne Hoover's maid, take care of Kazak. He threw raw meat down into the pit where Kazak lived in the daytime. He dragged Kazak into the pit at sunrise. He screamed at him and threw tennis balls at him at sundown. Then he turned him loose.

Benjamin Davis was first trumpet with the Midland City Symphony Orchestra, but he got no pay for that, so he needed a real job. He wore a thick gown made of war-surplus mattresses and chicken wire, so Kazak could not kill him. Kazak tried and tried. There were chunks of mattress and swatches of chicken wire all over the yard.

And Kazak did his best to kill anybody who came too close to the fence which enclosed his planet. He leaped at people as though the fence weren't there. The fence bellied out toward the sidewalk everywhere. It looked as though somebody had been shooting cannonballs at it from inside.

I should have noticed the queer shape of the fence when I got out of my automobile, when I did the *soigné* thing of lighting a cigarette. I should have known that a character as ferocious as Kazak was not easily cut out of a novel.

Kazak was crouching behind a pile of bronze pipe which the Maritimo Brothers had bought cheap from a hijacker earlier that day. Kazak meant to kill and *eat* me.

• • •

I turned my back to the fence, took a deep puff of my cigarette. *Pall Malls* would kill me by and by. And I mooned philosophically at the murky battlements of the old Keedsler Mansion, on the other side of Fairchild Boulevard.

Beatrice Keedsler had been raised in there. The most famous murders in the city's history had been committed there. Will Fairchild, the war hero, and the maternal uncle of Beatrice Keedsler, appeared one summer night in 1926 with a Springfield rifle. He shot and killed five relatives, three servants, two policemen, and all the animals in the Keedslers' private zoo. Then he shot himself through his heart.

When an autopsy was performed on him, a tumor the size of a piece of birdshot was found in his brain. This was what *caused* the murders.

• • •

After the Keedslers lost the mansion at the start of the Great Depression, Fred T. Barry and his parents moved in. The old place was filled with the sounds of British birds. It was silent property of the city now, and there was talk of making it into a museum where children could learn the history of Midland City—as told by arrowheads and stuffed animals and white men's early artifacts.

Fred T. Barry had offered to donate half a million dollars to the proposed museum, on one condition: that the first *Robo-Magic* and the early posters which advertised it be put on display.

And he wanted the exhibit to show, too, how machines evolved just as animals did, but with much greater speed.

• • •

I gazed at the Keedsler mansion, never dreaming that a volcanic dog was about to erupt behind me. Kilgore Trout came nearer. I was almost indifferent to his approach, although we had momentous things to say to one another about my having created him.

I thought instead of my paternal grandfather, who had been the first licensed architect in Indiana. He had designed some dream houses for *Hoosier* millionaires. They were mortuaries and guitar schools and cellar holes and parking lots now. I thought of my mother, who drove me around Indianapolis one time during the Great Depression, to impress me with how rich and powerful my maternal grandfather had been. She showed me where his brewery had been, where some of his dream houses had been. Every one of the monuments was a cellar hole.

Kilgore Trout was only half a block from his Creator now, and slowing down. I worried him.

I turned toward him, so that my sinus cavities, where all telepathic messages were sent and received, were lined up symmetrically with his. I told him this over and over telepathically: "I have good news for you."

Kazak sprung.

• • •

I saw Kazak out of the corner of my right eye. His eyes were pinwheels. His teeth were white daggers. His slobber was cyanide. His blood was nitroglycerine.

He was floating toward me like a zeppelin, hanging lazily in air.

My eyes told my mind about him.

My mind sent a message to my hypothalamus, told it to release the hormone CRF into the short vessels connecting my hypothalamus and my pituitary gland.

The CRF inspired my pituitary gland to dump the hormone ACTH into my bloodstream. My pituitary had been making and storing ACTH for just such an occasion. And nearer and nearer the zeppelin came.

And some of the ACTH in my bloodstream reached the outer shell of my adrenal gland, which had been making and storing glucocorticoids for emergencies. My adrenal gland added the glucocorticoids to my bloodstream. They went all over my body, changing glycogen into glucose. Glucose was muscle food. It would help me fight like a wildcat or run like a deer.

And nearer and nearer the zeppelin came.

My adrenal gland gave me a shot of adrenaline, too. I turned purple as my blood pressure skyrocketed. The adrenaline made my heart go like a burglar alarm. It also stood my hair on end. It also caused coagulants to pour into my bloodstream, so, in case I was wounded, my vital juices wouldn't drain away.

Everything my body had done so far fell within normal operating procedures for a human machine. But my body took one defensive measure which I am told was without precedent in medical history. It may have happened because some wire short-circuited or some gasket blew. At any rate, I also retracted my testicles into my abdominal cavity, pulled them into my fuselage like the landing gear of an airplane. And now they tell me that only surgery will bring them down again.

Be that as it may, Kilgore Trout watched me from half a block away, not knowing who I was, not knowing about Kazak and what my body had done about Kazak so far.

Trout had had a full day already, but it wasn't over yet. Now he saw his Creator leap completely over an automobile.

• • •

I landed on my hands and knees in the middle of Fairchild Boulevard.

Kazak was flung back by the fence. Gravity took charge of him as it had taken charge of me. Gravity slammed him down on concrete. Kazak was knocked silly.

Kilgore Trout turned away. He hastened anxiously back toward the hospital. I called out to him, but that only made him walk faster.

So I jumped into my car and chased him. I was still high as a kite on adrenaline and coagulants and all that. I did not know yet that I had retracted my testicles in all the excitement. I felt only vague discomfort down there.

Trout was cantering when I came alongside. I clocked him at eleven miles an hour, which was excellent for a man his age. He, too, was now full of adrenaline and coagulants and glucocorticoids.

My windows were rolled down, and I called this to him: "Whoa! Whoa! Mr. Trout! Whoa! Mr. Trout!"

It slowed him down to be called by name.

"Whoa! I'm a friend!" I said. He shuffled to a stop, leaned in panting exhaustion against a fence surrounding an appliance warehouse belonging to the General Electric Company. The company's monogram and motto hung in the night sky behind Kilgore Trout, whose eyes were wild. The motto was this:

PROGRESS IS OUR
MOST IMPORTANT PRODUCT

• • •

"Mr. Trout," I said from the unlighted interior of the car, "you have nothing to fear. I bring you tidings of great joy."

He was slow to get his breath back, so he wasn't much of a conversationalist at first. "Are—are you—from the—the Arts Festival?" he said. His eyes rolled and rolled.

"I am from the *Everything* Festival," I replied.

"The what?" he said.

I thought it would be a good idea to let him have a good look at me, and so attempted to flick on the dome light. I turned on the windshield washers instead. I turned them off again. My view of the lights of the County Hospital was garbled by beads of water. I pulled at another switch, and it came away in my hand. It was a cigarette lighter. So I had no choice but to continue to speak from darkness.

"Mr. Trout," I said, "I am a novelist, and I created you for use in my books."

"Pardon me?" he said.

"I'm your Creator," I said. "You're in the middle of a book right now—close to the end of it, actually."

"Um," he said.

"Are there any questions you'd like to ask?"

"Pardon me?" he said.

"Feel free to ask anything you want—about the past, about the future," I said. "There's a Nobel Prize in your future."

"A what?" he said.

"A Nobel Prize in medicine."

"Huh," he said. It was a noncommittal sound.

"I've also arranged for you to have a reputable publisher from now on. No more beaver books for you."

"Um," he said.

"If I were in your spot, I would certainly have lots of questions," I said.

"Do you have a gun?" he said.

I laughed there in the dark, tried to turn on the light again, activated the windshield washer again. "I don't need a gun to control you, Mr. Trout. All I have to do is write down something about you, and that's it."

• • •

"Are you *crazy*?" he said.

"No," I said. And I shattered his power to doubt me. I transported him to the Taj Mahal and then to Venice and then to Dar es Salaam and then to the surface of the Sun, where the flames could not consume him—and then back to Midland City again.

The poor old man crashed to his knees. He reminded me of the way my mother and Bunny Hoover's mother used to act whenever somebody tried to take their photographs.

As he cowered there, I transported him to the Bermuda of his childhood, had him contemplate the infertile egg of a Bermuda Ern. I took him from there to the Indianapolis of my childhood. I put him in a circus crowd there. I had him see a man with *locomotor ataxia* and a woman with a goiter as big as a zucchini.

• • •

I got out of my rented car. I did it noisily, so his ears would tell him a lot about his *Creator,* even if he was unwilling to use his eyes. I slammed the car door firmly. As I approached him from the driver's side of the car, I swiveled my feet some, so that my footsteps were not only deliberate but *gritty,* too.

I stopped with the tips of my shoes on the rim of the narrow field of his downcast eyes. "Mr. Trout, I love you," I said gently. "I have broken your mind to pieces. I want to make it whole. I want you to feel a wholeness and inner harmony such as I have never allowed you to feel before. I want you to raise your eyes, to look at what I have in my hand."

I had nothing in my hand, but such was my power over Trout that he would see in it whatever I wished him to see. I might have shown him a Helen of Troy, for instance, only six inches tall.

"Mr. Trout—*Kilgore*—" I said, "I hold in my hand a symbol of wholeness and harmony and nourishment. It is Oriental in its simplicity, but we are *Americans,* Kilgore, and not Chinamen. We Americans require symbols which are richly colored and three-dimensional and juicy. Most of all, we hunger for symbols which have not been poisoned by great sins our nation has committed, such as slavery and genocide and criminal neglect, or by tinhorn commercial greed and cunning.

"Look up, Mr. Trout," I said, and I waited patiently. "Kilgore—?"

The old man looked up, and he had my father's wasted face when my father was a widower—when my father was an old old man.

He saw that I held an apple in my hand.

• • •

"I am approaching my fiftieth birthday, Mr. Trout," I said. "I am cleansing and renewing myself for the very different sorts of years to come. Under similar spiritual conditions, Count Tolstoi freed his serfs. Thomas Jefferson freed his slaves. I am going to set at liberty all the literary characters who have served me so loyally during my writing career.

"You are the only one I am telling. For the others, tonight will be a night like any other night. Arise, Mr. Trout, you are free, you are *free*."

He arose shamblingly.

I might have shaken his hand, but his right hand was injured, so our hands remained dangling at our sides.

"*Bon voyage,*" I said. I disappeared.

• • •

I somersaulted lazily and pleasantly through the void, which is my hiding place when I dematerialize. Trout's cries to me faded as the distance between us increased.

His voice was my father's voice. I *heard* my father—and I

saw my mother in the void. My mother stayed far, far away, because she had left me a legacy of suicide.

A small hand mirror floated by. It was a *leak* with a mother-of-pearl handle and frame. I captured it easily, held it up to my own right eye, which looked like this:

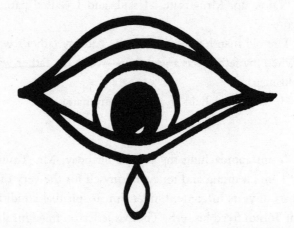

Here was what Kilgore Trout cried out to me in my father's voice: "*Make me young, make me young, make me young!*"

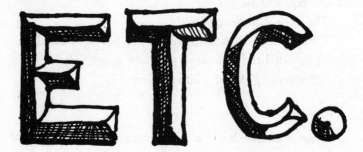

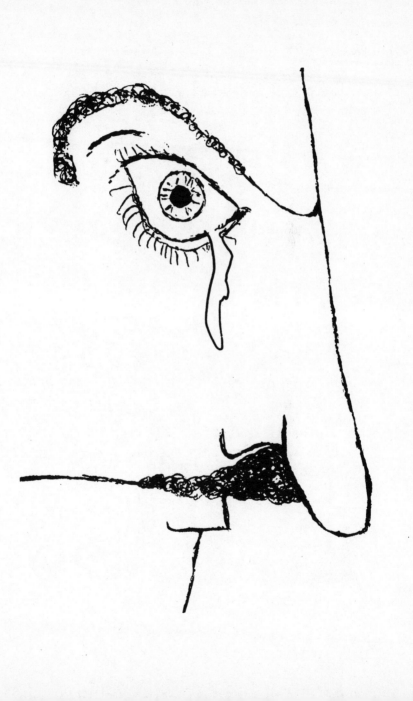

KURT **V**ONNEGUT, **J**R., is the son and grandson of Indianapolis architects. They were painters, too. His only living sibling is a distinguished physicist who discovered, among other things, that silver iodide can sometimes make it snow or rain. This is Mr. Vonnegut's seventh novel. He wrote it mostly in New York City. His six children are full-grown.